The Eyes of a Phantom

Erica Lee Cooke

This is a work of fiction. Names, characters, businesses, places, events, and incidents are either the products of the author's imagination or used in a fictitious manner. Any resemblance to actual persons, living or dead, or actual events is purely coincidental.

Copyright © 2017 Erica Lee Cooke
All rights reserved.
ISBN: 0998156655
ISBN-13: 978-0998156651

More By Erica Lee Cooke

The Eyes of a Phantom Trilogy
#1: The Eyes of a Phantom
#2: The Eyes to the Soul (coming soon)
#3: The Eyes of the Beholder (coming soon)

Supernaturally Bound Series
#1: Secrets Abound
#2: Unbound
#3: Enemies Abound
#4: Bound by Honesty (coming soon)
#5: Bound by Fate (coming soon)

For more information on
Erica Lee Cooke's books, visit
www.EricaLeeCooke.com

.

CHAPTER ONE

SECRETS LEFT BEHIND

"Elizabeth, honey, we're almost there." I heard Mom's voice cut through the haze of my dream. I opened my eyes and instantly felt the repercussions of sleeping in such an awkward position. My neck ached and my leg had fallen asleep. "Were you having another nightmare?" Mom asked.

"No," I replied.

She pressed her lips together tightly but didn't call me out on the obvious lie. I was grateful that this nine-hour drive was coming to an end. I glanced at the sign that read "Welcome to Middleton" and my stomach dropped. Middleton, Idaho – aka, my new home. Dread gripped me, but I knew this was the only option I had left. It was either move in with my Aunt Meredith or continue living as a pariah back in Oregon.

"How much does Aunt Meredith know

about what happened?" I questioned, picking at some leftover nail polish on my thumb from weeks ago – a spa session that acted as Mom's last attempt at cheering me up.

"Very little. I thought that was best. She just knows you've been having a hard time since the accident," my mother explained.

"Does she know the accident was my fault?" I bit the inside of my cheek as old guilt filled me.

"Honey, it wasn't entirely your fault. It wasn't even mostly your fault. Tray made the decision to drive that night; you didn't force him to. People just need someone to blame," she consoled. I'd heard this speech countless times over this past summer.

I nodded but didn't actually agree with her. She didn't know the whole story. Sure, I got that everyone at my old high school were all hypocrites. Ninety percent of them had been driving drunk, too. But they weren't altogether wrong in blaming me for Tray's death. *I* had been the one to get into a fight with Amanda, my best friend, who was supposed to be our designated driver that night. *I* was the one who wanted to leave her behind. That was the only reason Tray had been driving that night. Tray would still be alive if I had just let Amanda drive.

I frowned as I stared out the window. Everyone hated me after that night. Tray had been the star quarterback and, therefore, the star of the town. I had basically been run off with pitch forks.

Great way to end my junior year.

I forcefully shoved the unwanted memories to the back of my mind. The accident was months ago, but it still felt fresh. This was supposed to be a clean slate for me. That would never happen if I couldn't stop thinking about it. I inhaled deeply and turned my attention back to Mom.

"So, Middleton has a six thousand population, now? It's really growing. Soon, you won't even miss it with a blink of an eye," I commented. I had visited Aunt Meredith as a child, and I mostly just remembered the sheer boredom of the small-town life.

"Listen, Aunt Meredith is doing us a huge favor by taking you in for your last year of high school. I do *not* want to hear any more of your rude comments about Middleton. Do you understand me, young lady?" Mom's words were stern, much like the expression that currently adorned her face.

"Yes, ma'am." I knew this was going to put

Aunt Meredith out. She was sort of an old maid, but she preferred it that way. She was nice enough, but she loved being by herself. This would be an adjustment for the both of us. My plan was to stay out the way as much as possible. That included at school. I wasn't here to make friends or be sucked into the social scene. I just wanted to graduate and move far, far away. Unfortunately, Mom was not on board with my plans.

"Aunt Meredith was telling me about Middleton's football team. She said they're national champions three years running," Mom said in a hinting tone. I nodded as I stared out the window. She continued, "She also said they have a great cheerleading squad."

"Good for them." I was *so* not interested in joining another cheer squad.

"Come on, honey. I think it would be good for you. The doctor said your leg is back to perfect condition. Get back on the horse. You loved cheerleading before the accident," she encouraged.

"Yeah, *before* the accident. *Before* they all turned against me. I don't know if you remember, but my old squad led the pack of torch-bearing villagers." I twisted my hand into a tight fist allowing my nails to sink into the skin of my palm. Their betrayal still stung. *Some sisterhood.* I had lost my boyfriend and instead of helping me through it, they pointed fingers.

"It'll be different here," she assured. Her worried expression made me take a mental step back. I knew this was just as hard on her. I didn't have to make it even harder.

"I know, Mom. I'll give it a shot." I gave a small smile which seemed to soothe part of her anxiety.

We pulled up to an older house with chipped paint and an overgrown lawn. Mom had volunteered me to help with outside work that my aunt couldn't do. I hadn't realized how much work that actually would be.

Oh, well, I did say I wanted a distraction.

"Are you ready?" Mom drew my attention back.

"As ready as I'll ever be."

We knocked on the front door and heard Aunt Meredith ordering her cats – she had three – to get back. The door flung open and she greeted us with a warm smile. She was a round woman which made my mother appear even thinner. A stranger would be hard-pressed to believe the two were sisters. My mother was a good foot taller than my aunt. It wasn't just the physicality of the two that was different. Their personalities were on opposite sides of the spectrum. My mom was very outspoken and assertive where my aunt was soft-spoken and timid. Perhaps, that bred from my mother being the older of the two. I wouldn't know about sibling dynamics, being an only child and all.

"Katie! Beth! How was the trip?" Aunt Meredith asked as she pet the fur ball she was holding in her left arm. I studied the room as Mom told Aunt Meredith all about the car ride over. It was just as I remembered. Cat figurines covered the fire mantel. An old portrait of Aunt Meredith and Mom as children with their parents hung on the wall. The house was well maintained – on the inside at least – considering it was over a hundred years old.

"Beth, dear, you'll be staying in the guest room upstairs." Aunt Meredith's words tugged me back into the conversation.

"Okay, thank you. I'll go unpack." I excused myself and headed up the stairs. My room was small, but it had its own bathroom. I was grateful for the privacy that would bring.

As I unpacked, I wondered what my new school would be like. I told myself it didn't matter since I'd only be here a year, but my curiosity still steered my thoughts.

"Knock, knock." Mom peeked her head into the room. "I'm leaving soon." Loneliness planted itself inside of me. I wished Mom could stay the night, but she had to work in the morning. I already missed her. She must have seen my eyes water because she wrapped her arms around me in a tight hug. "I know this is hard, but it really is for the best. Your dad and I will visit as often as we can." I nodded but remained silent for fear the tears would fall. "I want you to promise me something, okay?"

"What is it?" I asked in a small voice. I hated how childlike I sounded at the moment.

"I want you to genuinely *try* to start over here. Don't just go through the motions. Make some friends, try out for cheerleading, the whole nine yards." She stroked my hair as she spoke. What she asked of me went against my whole plan, but I knew it would ease her mind to hear.

"I promise I'll *try*," I said slowly.

"I love you, baby." She squeezed me tighter. "This is going to be good for you," she said more to herself than to me.

"I love you, too."

The next morning, I woke up extra early.

School was less than a week away, and I decided I would keep myself busy by working on the yard. I threw on some old jeans and pulled my long, brown hair into a tight ponytail. When I left, Aunt Meredith was still in her room asleep. It was about a mile to the local hardware store, but I didn't mind the walk. I enjoyed the exercise, and it helped to clear my mind.

The store wasn't as large as I remembered it being. But, then again, I had been much smaller back then. I picked out a weed eater and some lawn fertilizer. I knew Aunt Meredith had an old lawn mower in the storage building behind the house. Whether it still worked was another story, but it was one I'd deal with later. I considered picking up some paint for the house, too, but as I stared at the options, I wasn't sure what Aunt Meredith would want.

"Need help?" I heard someone say from behind me.

"Um, no, I'm good." I turned to see a guy about my age. He was cute and his body told me he was an athlete. He had a fresh tan from the summer, and his dark brown hair hung slightly in his grayish blue eyes, but it didn't seem to bother him. His smile showed off two dimples, one in each cheek.

"Doing some last minute yard work?" He gestured toward my selection of items.

"Yeah," I answered. I glanced down and noticed he wasn't wearing the store's uniform. "Do you even work here?"

"No, I just saw a pretty girl who looked like she was in need of some help. So I thought I'd offer." He continued smiling as he leaned his shoulder against a shelf. "My name's Jason."

"Beth," I responded. I had to admit, he was attractive, but I was sticking to my guns on the *no socializing* thing.

"Are you new to town? I don't think I've seen you around." He cocked his head to the side with a slight gleam in his eye.

"Yeah, I just moved in with my aunt," I answered, still browsing the various colors provided by the paint swatches. I spotted a couple of off-white colors that seemed close to the original paint.

"Oh, what's her name?" he questioned.

"Meredith Vaughn," I answered and wasn't surprised when his expression told that he recognized the name. Everyone knew everyone in a small town like Middleton.

"Yeah, I know her. My mom actually manages to get Meredith out of the house every once in a while," he told me.

This time I *was* surprised.

"Wow, that's quite an accomplishment." My voice sounded slightly awed. "Your mom must be pretty great."

"She is. You'll get to see soon enough. She coaches the cheerleading squad," he announced.

"What makes you think I'm joining the squad?" My eyebrows shot up at his assumption.

"I'm the star quarterback. I know a cheerleader when I see one." He smirked. I could feel my face drop. My sense of déjà vu was overpowering. Of all the guys to run into, it had to be the football team's quarterback. It was as if karma absolutely refused to let me forget what had happened. His expression turned confused. "Hey, I was just kidding. I guess I'm not on my game today."

"No, it's fine. I just have to go. I have a lot of work to do," I told him as I grabbed a few of the paint swatches so I could have Aunt Meredith pick a color later.

"Oh, right, okay. I guess I'll see you at school. You are going to school here, right?" He smiled again, but this time it wasn't quite as arrogant.

"Yeah, senior year," I said.

"See you Monday, then," he said before disappearing down the aisle.

By the time the Sunday before school rolled around, I had the outside of the house looking kempt. I wasn't exactly a landscaper, but I knew how to use a lawnmower and a weed eater. I was feeling pretty good about my work when I lay in bed that night. All feelings of contentment flew out the window the moment I began dreaming. Flashes of Tray's bloodied face were painted in the portraits of my mind. I awoke with guilty tears streaming down my face.

I wondered if this would ever get better. It had been months and I still had nightmares about the crash, about Tray's death. I didn't know if I even deserved for it to get better. Tray was dead because of a petty fight I'd had with Amanda. Amanda never let me forget it, either. She'd told everyone who would listen that I was to blame. That if it hadn't been for me, *she* would have been driving that night.

With a frustrated sigh, I tossed my covers over to the side of the bed. Light barely trickled in through the window, so I knew it was still early. After my shower, I had plenty of time to kill, so I cleaned up around the house in an attempt to make my presence more convenient for Aunt Meredith. I would have made her breakfast, but I knew she wouldn't be awake for a couple more hours, and I'd be long gone to school. I poured some coffee into a disposable, paper cup my aunt had stacks of. It appeared she bought everything in bulk at Costco.

The walk to school only consisted of five blocks and, therefore, took hardly any time at all. I stepped into the deserted school. I had planned to leave early so I could get my schedule from the office and maybe take a stroll around to find my classes. Unfortunately, the school had been much closer to my aunt's house than I had expected. The office was not open yet, so I decided to start my tour early.

I found what appeared to be the senior hall and made note of the progression of locker numbers. If I had a number close to 800, then it would be near the end door. After a few minutes of mindless wandering, I found myself at the football field outside. The football team was having practice and I could hear the coach screaming a myriad of demeaning statements that were meant to somehow encourage the team. I watched from behind the chain link fence.

I wondered which number Jason was. They all had their helmets on, so I couldn't tell who was who. Not that I knew anyone other than Jason. I wasn't even sure why I cared. I *was not* going to date anyone, not even a blue-eyed cutie. It wasn't happening.

I sighed and took a step back. This wasn't my scene anymore. I couldn't be that peppy cheerleader that I'd been four months ago. Too much had changed.

The office was open when I made my way back over to it. My schedule was as plain as I could have gotten. No yearbook, no cheerleading, nothing extra. I signed up for the required classes and that was it. This had me getting out of school early every day with the condition that I was to get a part-time job.

My first two classes went smoothly. I sat in the far back and managed to be invisible. Some students noticed I was new but seemed to pick up on my *don't talk to me* vibe. Which is why I was shocked when I heard someone call my name out as I made my way to my locker.

"Beth!" I heard the male voice shout again. I turned to see Jason who caught up to me. He fell into pace beside me as I continued my original path. Once we got to my locker he said, "I saw you watching us practice this morning."

Embarrassment flushed my face. "I wasn't-"

His laughter cut me off. "You're really cute when you're embarrassed, you know that?"

He reached over and tucked a loose strand of hair behind my ear causing a small flutter in my chest. I forced my heart to quit its rogue feelings of excitement and was about to argue with his flirtatious statement when I noticed someone across the hall. He watched our entire encounter without any qualms over his open staring. He casually leaned against the wall with his arms crossed over his muscled chest. He had light brown hair that was shaggy with a slight curl to it. He had blue eyes that were bright, where Jason's were more of a smoky blue. His cheekbones were high and his mouth was set firm. His physique screamed athlete while his demeanor cried loner.

"Beth, did you hear me?" Jason waved his hand in front of my face.

"I'm sorry, what?" I asked having completely missed everything he'd just said.

"I was asking you if you wanted to go see a movie tomorrow night," he repeated.

"Actually, I kind of already have plans. Maybe some other time." I tried to be polite as I brushed him off.

"Sure, some other time, then." He gave me

one last smile before he morphed into the crowd of students. I glanced back over to the now empty wall where loner boy had been standing. Something seemed vaguely familiar about him, but I couldn't quite put my finger on it. I shook it off as I closed my locker. No one spoke to me for the rest of the day. I spotted a couple of cheerleaders wearing their uniforms around school. It felt strange to not be involved in all things pep. I ignored any residual pleasant feelings I had toward cheerleading and walked to my aunt's house. I mean, *my house*.

The next few days were nearly identical to that first one, minus Jason asking me out. He still smiled and said hello but didn't attempt to land a date with me again. At home, the house was quiet except for the cats' small shuffling noises. When the house phone rang, I was startled. I raced over to the phone hoping it would be my mom. It was.

"Hey, baby. How are things going?" She spoke low and I knew she was at work. I twisted the spiraled cord in my hand as I soaked in every octave of her voice. I hadn't let myself feel the homesickness that had nestled inside my stomach until this moment.

"Good." I bit my lip to hold it together. I didn't want her to hear how upset I was.

"Have you made any friends?"

"Well, um, sort of," I muttered.

"Lizzie…" Mom's voice bled disappointment. I hadn't gone by Lizzie since I was twelve. Mom was the only one allowed to call me that, now.

"I'm sorry; it's just hard. Everyone already has their clicks. It's senior year. These people have known each other since birth. There's not really room for a new person." I stared down at my shoes as silence met me on the other end of the line. "Mom?"

"Yes, I'm here." She let out a sigh. "I thought you said you would try."

"I will… I am," I lied.

"Well, Aunt Meredith says the first football game of the season is a home game. She said it's tomorrow night. You should go," she insisted.

"I don't know," I murmured.

"That wasn't a request. I am still your mother and I am telling you to go to that game tomorrow. Check out the cheerleading squad and talk to a few people. Understood?" Her tone told me there was no room for argument.

"Yes, I understand." I rolled my eyes.

"Do not roll your eyes at me, young lady," Mom barked.

"Ugh, I didn't-" I began to lie.

"Don't lie. I am your mother and I know everything," she asserted.

"I'm sorry." I didn't know why I was surprised. My mom had always had eyes in the back of her head. Now, she apparently had eyes in Middleton, as well.

"I love you, baby. I just want you to be happy. I honestly believe that all starts with this football game." Her tone was soft.

"I love you, too." We hung up with promises to talk soon. I set the phone back on the hook. I had to use the landline because my mom had taken my cell phone away and forced me to shut down all my social media accounts when the bullying got bad. I didn't really miss it if I was being honest. It was interesting how clear minded you became once you took the phone away from your face.

I thought about what Mom had said. She seemed pretty hard-set in her belief that if I just made a friend, things would get better for me. Maybe she was right. She usually was. What would it hurt to check out the game?

CHAPTER TWO

SECRETLY WATCHING

The football game was nearly to halftime when I wandered through the bleachers in search of a seat. The crowd roared with excitement as the warm night air carried scents of popcorn and nachos. My stomach growled, but I wasn't a fan of concession stand food.

My eyes scanned the football field until I spotted Jason. I had found out he was number 22 at the pep rally that had been held earlier in the day. He wasn't kidding about being the star of the team. He threw the football further than any other quarterback I'd ever seen. It was impressive. The crowd agreed with my sentiment as they cheered for him with great enthusiasm.

My eyes drifted from the field to the crowd. It seemed the whole town was here, all sporting the Vikings' team colors of navy and gold. I glanced down at my red tank top and realized I stood out. My thoughts were stopped in their tracks when I spotted loner boy standing near the chain link fence. He was watching the game, but then, as if he could feel my eyes, he looked up directly at me. My face burned red as I quickly moved my eyes away. After a few moments, I dared a peek at him. He was still staring at me. *What was with this guy?* A chill ran down my spine at his persistent staring.

The crowd made a unison, gasping noise. My eyes darted back to the field, curious what had caused the reaction. Jason was down on the ground. I had missed the details, but from what I could gather, he had been tackled and was apparently injured. A couple of guys helped him limp off the field. It appeared he had twisted his ankle.

I dragged my eyes back to loner boy. He continued to watch me. I felt uneasy under his gaze, so I decided I'd fulfill my mom's other request. I went to check out the cheerleading squad. I observed their cheering for a few minutes, but the sharp, stabbing feeling I felt in my chest as they reminded me of my old squad told me this was not going to happen. I let out a long sigh and decided it was time to leave. I moseyed to the nearest exit which took me past the locker rooms.

"Beth!" I twisted around to see Jason closing the distance between us. "Are you leaving?" He sounded disappointed.

"Yeah," I answered without explanation. "How's your ankle?"

"Good. It just needed to be iced." He grinned.

"That's good," I said awkwardly.

He paused before asking, "Do you want to grab some coffee tomorrow?"

"I don't know," I hesitated. Mom wanted me to make friends, but I wasn't sure I was up for it.

"Come on. It's just coffee," he maintained.

"Alright. Pick me up at six." I smiled.

"Yes! I knew you wouldn't be able to resist me," he joked. I laughed with a shake of my head. "Well, I've got a game to win." He strolled off toward the field and I could hear the crowd roar in response. Jason was certainly arrogant, but I guess he had good reason to be. He was hot and amazing at football. I just hoped he wasn't *too* arrogant.

I turned the corner and saw loner boy staring at me from under the bleachers. *What the hell?* Was he following me? I decided to confront him and crossed under the bleachers until I stood directly in front of him.

"What's your problem?" I asked expectantly. His eyes grew wide in surprise. I wondered if I was the first person to confront the creep. If he thought I was scared of him, he had another thing coming. "What is with the staring? It's rude and creepy." He regarded me in silence. "Well?" When he still didn't respond, I muttered, "whatever" and left. I could feel his eyes boring into my back until I was out of his view.

What a freak! He probably got off on making people feel uncomfortable.

The next day, I spent the morning and most of the afternoon painting the outside of the house. Aunt Meredith had decided to stick with the original color. She wasn't a woman of change. I managed to get the first layer of paint finished before I had to shower for my coffee date.

I scrubbed the dried paint off my skin while I stood under the hot water. The bathroom was filled with steam by the time my shower ended. I still had a smudge of paint on the back of my neck, but I figured I'd just wear my hair down. I wrapped a towel around my body and stepped into my bedroom. My heart leapt in my chest when I saw loner boy *in my room*.

"What the hell are you doing in here?" I

screamed at him.

"You need to stay away from Jason," he stated without answering my question.

"*You* need to get out of my house! Now!" I yelled. My heart raced as I realized Aunt Meredith had made a trip to Nampa for her weekly Costco shopping. I was home alone. "I'm going to call the cops."

"You don't want to do that," he warned. The words seemed threatening, but his tone didn't.

"Yeah, I think I do." My voice was smooth, not letting on how fearful I was. He didn't move. My eyes bounced around the room in search of a weapon. The only thing I had that might even remotely do some damage was a high-heeled shoe, but it was in my closet.

"Jason's not who you think he is," loner boy asserted.

"I don't *think* he is anyone. I barely even know him," I countered. "Look, if that's what you came to tell me, then you've said it and you can go." I glared at him as I pulled the towel tighter around me afraid it would fall. Relief flooded me as he strolled through my doorway.

"Bye, Lizzie," he threw over his shoulder as he left.

"Why did you call me that?" I asked after him but there was no response. I raced down the stairs to catch him, but he was already gone.

Nobody calls me Lizzie, I thought to myself. Especially not someone I *just* met. This guy was creeping me out more and more with each encounter.

I brushed off the eerie feeling loner boy had left me with and prepared for my date. I straightened my hair and put on a small amount of makeup. I browsed through my clothes, searching for an outfit. It was hot outside, so I decided to wear shorts and a tank top. All my tank tops had at least a one inch thick strap so as to cover up my scar. I traced my finger along the thin, vertical line that ran from my chest to my right shoulder. The skin still had a phantom tenderness to it although it had long healed.

The sound of a knock snapped me from my trance. Jason was right on time. I grabbed my handbag and shot down the stairs. Jason wore dark jeans with a checkered, button-up shirt. Its sleeves were folded up to his elbows. A smile grew across his face when his eyes met mine.

"Are you ready?" he asked.

"Yeah."

Even though the coffee house was close

enough to walk to, we drove over to it in Jason's red jeep. He told me about how his father bought it for him when the team won nationals last year. I feigned interest, but my mind was back on loner boy. He had called me *Lizzie* like he knew me. I supposed his unexpected bedroom visit should have been the part to shake me the most, but it wasn't. Don't get me wrong; that part was creepy to the core, but there was something familiar about him that I couldn't shake.

"Earth to Beth." Jason's voice rattled through my thoughts. I glanced up and saw that we were no longer moving. "We're here."

I smiled and followed his lead by exiting the jeep. We entered the tiny coffee shop that looked like it wanted to be a Starbucks when it grew up. The thick aroma of coffee brewing filled my nose. I grinned at the sudden flash of memories flooding my brain. Coffee always reminded me of Mom. She was a straight-up addict, so the house always smelled of coffee in the morning and most evenings. I ignored the tinge of homesickness that followed suit behind the memory.

I spotted a 'now hiring' sign on the counter and made a mental note to grab an application before I left. If I had to get a part-time job for school anyway, it might as well be one that was filled with happy memory triggering smells. After ordering my vanilla latte and Jason's black coffee, we sat at a tall, round table that needed stools to reach it.

"So, did you guys win the game?" I asked, searching for some topic of conversation.

"Of course." His grin was arrogant, but his dimples made him appear innocent enough to counteract it. "We beat them fourteen to seven."

"Impressive. I guess your twisted ankle didn't slow you down any," I pointed out.

"Nah, like I said, it just needed a little ice." He smirked. After a moment, his expression changed to serious. "So, I've been curious about something."

"And what is that?" I took a small sip of my latte.

"Why did you move in with your aunt? I mean, it seems crazy to change schools for your senior year." His eyes watched for my reaction. I put every ounce of effort I could into keeping my expression smooth. One of my fears coming here was that my past would somehow follow me. Without social media, it would be difficult for it to do so, unless I slipped up. I apparently was silent for too long because Jason continued on, "Was it a bad breakup? Is that why you seemed freaked out when I asked you on a date?"

"Something like that." It was close to the truth. Of course, the bad breakup was between me and my entire high school. Eh, semantics.

"It must have been really bad for you to move like that," he pointed out. I panicked as his interest grew. The last thing I needed was for someone to go poking around my past.

"It wasn't a bad breakup. My parents are going through a rough patch. They need some alone time to work things out, so I volunteered to stay with Aunt Meredith for a while," I lied as smoothly as I could.

"How selfless of you." He smiled. I couldn't tell if he entirely bought it, but at least he dropped the subject.

As I lifted my cup to my lips, a few drops of hot coffee spilled onto my chest near my shoulder. "Ouch," I exclaimed. Jason quickly grabbed a couple of napkins and dabbed them onto the droplets.

"What's that from?" His eyes widened. His movements had caused my strap to fall to the side, exposing my scar. His hand froze as he stared at it. I wondered if he was as shallow as he was arrogant.

"I don't remember. It happened when I was

a child. I probably fell or something." I swiftly moved my strap back into place. Something strange beamed from his eyes as his mind seemed to race.

"How old were you?" he asked with an overwhelming interest I didn't understand.

"I literally have no memory of it, so I couldn't say. Pretty young." I suddenly felt incredibly uncomfortable.

He seemed to notice the change in me. "Sorry, I didn't mean to pry. I just think scars are interesting. It's like a diary or something."

"Yeah, well, I'm not a fan of people reading my diary," I asserted.

"Good point." He took a drink of his coffee, but his eyes lingered on the now covered scar.

What was his fascination?

"So, have you applied for any universities, yet?" I was desperate to change the subject.

"Yeah, a few of them are trying to scout me, but I haven't decided on one yet. Have you thought about where you're going?"

"I'm thinking Florida." I flashed a smile.

"Love the beach?" He lifted a brow. "Or is it the three thousand miles away part that is appealing to you?"

"A little of both." Okay, mostly the latter, but I *did* enjoy the beach. Who wouldn't want to spend their college years with an amazing tan?

"Hey, Jason," I heard a feminine voice say from behind me. I glanced over my shoulder and saw two girls I recognized from the cheer squad waltz over to our table. They slid onto the two empty stools. "Who's this?"

"This is Beth. Beth, this is Kathy and Stephanie," Jason introduced. The girls studied me momentarily. They both had bright blond hair pulled back into high ponytails.

"Nice to meet you," Kathy said with a fake smile. She turned back to Jason. "So, are you coming to Tory's party tonight?"

"I wasn't really planning on it." His eyes met mine. "I'm kind of in the middle of something."

"So, bring her." Kathy shrugged.

"Do you want to go?" he asked. I could tell he hoped I'd say yes. The truth of the matter settled over me in a layer of realization. We were just not compatible. Me from six months ago? Yeah, that chick would be all over Jason. Her whole life revolved around football games and parties, too. Me now? Not so much.

"No, but you go ahead. I kind of want to talk to the manager here about a job. I have less than a week to find one for school," I explained.

"Are you sure?"

"Yeah, it's fine," I assured.

"See? She said it's fine. Now, let's go before all the good alcohol is gone," Kathy insisted.

Jason gave me a brief hug before they shuffled out the door. I headed to the counter and asked if the manager was in. I was told to fill out an application and wait at the table in the corner. The application didn't take long to fill out since I'd only had one other job and that was at my mom's office as a temp.

"Hi, my name's Susan," said a tall, thin woman that appeared to be in her mid-thirties as she offered her hand for me to shake.

"Beth Michaels." I accepted the handshake. Susan slid into the seat across from mine. I handed her my application and she scanned through it. I began babbling while she did so. "I just moved here. I need to get a job for school. Not that I don't want the job anyway, but it's a condition of my school schedule. Even if it wasn't, though, I'd still want to work here. It reminds me of home."

She smiled at my ramblings. "Home?"

"Well, my mom. She loves coffee. I just moved in with my aunt, so the smell eases the homesickness." I smiled hoping I wasn't oversharing. Susan didn't seem to mind.

"Well, I'm glad to hear that." She paused in contemplation. "I think you'd be perfect for the job. I'd like you to start tomorrow if you could."

"Yeah, that'd be great," I said enthusiastically.

"I do need to warn you of something, though." Her eyes narrowed.

"Alright."

"You'd be in a bit of a precarious situation," she said. "The girl you're replacing died about six months ago. I tried to hold off on replacing her out of respect, but I just can't handle all the extra hours anymore. The reason I bring it up is that the other girls are still... sensitive to the subject. They aren't exactly happy about me hiring someone new. They'll come around, eventually."

I didn't know what to say to that. *The girl had died?* I wasn't sure it was smart of me to put myself in a position to become a pariah again, but I *really* wanted this job. I nodded and she smiled.

"Good. Well, come by around one and we'll start your training. It was really nice meeting you, Beth." She shook my hand, once again.

"You too," I replied. I began to leave but twisted around as a thought occurred to me.

"How did she die?"

I could tell the question made her uncomfortable and I instantly regretted asking. "She was murdered."

"Oh." That was all I could say. I hadn't expected that answer. I thought maybe a car wreck or a hiking accident or *anything else*. I never thought of Middleton as anything but safe. I knew this was pushing the limits, but I had to know. "Did they catch the killer?"

"No." Susan frowned. She quickly disappeared behind the counter after that. She definitely did not feel comfortable speaking about the incident.

"You sort of look like her, you know?" said the girl at the counter.

"I'm sorry?" I wasn't sure what she was talking about.

"Emily, the girl that was killed. You look like her," she explained. She had clearly overheard my conversation with Susan. I didn't respond to the strange observation. A feeling of foreboding settled over me. I had absolutely no connection to that girl, I reminded myself. Something felt so off about it, though. I felt the barista's eyes burn the skin on the back of my neck as I exited into the night.

As I strolled the route that led me home, my mind was heavy in thought. A girl had been murdered? *In Middleton?* There was no way I was going to tell my mom about this. She would make me pack up and move in with Aunt Leslie. No way in hell was I moving in with that mommy dearest reincarnate. She raised her kids to be robots. I loved my cousins, but they were brainwashed. No, Aunt Meredith was my only acceptable option. Obviously, Aunt Meredith wasn't worried about it or she would have told Mom. My train of thought was lost as a feeling of being watched wiggled into my brain. I glanced around and spotted loner boy leaning against the corner of a white picket fence.

My eyes met his as mine narrowed into a glare. "Why are you following me?" I yelled at him as I rushed over to where he stood. He quickly disappeared around the corner. Only a moment later, I turned the corner to see an empty street. I grunted in frustration.

Great, some girl that looked like me was murdered and now I had a stalker. I prayed they weren't somehow connected. Leave it to me to catch the attention of the town psycho.

CHAPTER THREE

SECRETS MISSING

Sleep evaded me for most of the night. So much was on my mind that, at one point, I thought for sure it would erupt like a volcano and spew my musings all over the bedroom walls. Of course, that didn't happen. When I awoke the next morning, the walls were still the same old peach color they'd always been. I rolled over in hopes of catching a couple more hours of shut eye before work, but the sound of laughter traveled from downstairs and piqued my interest.

As I breezed down the steps, I could hear more of the conversation and realized Aunt Meredith was on the phone. I heard her say my name and knew she was speaking with Mom about me. Her smile grew when she spotted me.

"Yeah, Beth's right here. Did you want to talk to her?" Mom must have said yes because she handed me the phone.

"Hi, honey. How are you doing?" She

sounded chipper.

"Good. How are you?" I asked, even though her good mood was clear.

"I'm good, baby. How was the football game?" she asked. "Did you check out the cheer squad?"

"I did." I breathed. "I just can't, Mom. And before you get mad, I went on a date last night."

"You did?" I could hear the smile in her words. "How did it go?"

"It was okay. I think we'll probably just be friends, but that's okay. Oh, and I got a job at a coffee house," I told her.

"That's awesome. What about school? Have you joined any clubs? Did you join yearbook?"

"Well, no, but…" I began.

"Honey, I want you to get more involved. Just think about it, the busier you keep yourself, the faster the school year will go," she insisted.

"My shift is starting soon. I have to get ready. Love you, Mom." I handed the phone back to Aunt Meredith. My mom was the pushiest person I knew. I knew she pushed me because she wanted the best for me, but she never could figure out that, sometimes, I just needed to be left alone. I raced upstairs to make my lie believable. I knew Aunt Meredith reported my every move to

Mom. Not that I could blame her. Mom was a hard woman to say no to. That's what made Mom an awesome realtor.

I dressed in a pair of dark blue jeans and a black t-shirt that was the coffee shop's uniform, tied my hair in a ponytail, and darted out the front door. I wasn't sure how I was planning to kill the three hours before work, but I knew I'd figure it out. I wandered aimlessly around town until I found myself at a tiny creek. A broad tree offered shade from the beating sun, so I sprawled out on the ground beneath it. I remembered this place from years ago. I played here for most of the summer when I was seven. Aunt Meredith had been having medical problems. We stayed with her for the summer so that Mom could help out.

"So, you remember this place, but you don't remember me?" I heard a male voice say. When I opened my eyes, I spotted loner boy leaning against the tree as he watched me.

"Excuse me?" I propped myself up onto my elbow so I could see him better.

"You don't remember me, do you?" he asked with an amused expression.

"I don't... know," I muttered. There was something familiar about him, but the memory refused to surface.

"I thought all girls remembered their first kiss." He grinned. The memory slammed into me like a freight train.

"Jared?" Suddenly, it seemed obvious. His bright blue eyes and the single curl that fell to his forehead. Jared and I played together that summer I stayed in Middleton. One day, we were picking flowers and he snuck a kiss. Why had that been so hard for me to recall?

"Took you long enough." He slid down the tree until he sat at its base.

"Well, you're ten years older with a lot less baby fat," I argued.

"I remembered you." His eyes held onto mine.

"How'd you recognize me?" I lifted a brow in disbelief.

"You have the same smile." He grinned. "And the same glare."

"Then why didn't you just tell me who you were instead of following me around and acting like a creeper?" I frowned.

"I wasn't following you around. It's a small town," he defended.

"Yeah, small town, small bedroom," I shot.

"I didn't mean to scare you. The door was

unlocked, so I came in. I just wanted to warn you away from Jason." He rubbed the back of his head and, as he did, his shirt contoured to the muscles of his arm.

"I could have figured out Jason was arrogant all on my own. I'm not a little girl anymore," I asserted. His eyes dragged over my body and his expression seemed to agree with my statement.

"So, you won't go out with him again?" His eyes met mine.

"No, our date didn't exactly go well." I pulled a blade of grass out of the ground and twirled it between my finger and thumb.

"That's good," he said.

"Not sure my mom would agree with you." I bit my lip.

"Yeah, well, your mom doesn't know Jason," he asserted.

"And what is it that she doesn't know about him, exactly?" I quirked a brow at him. I began to suspect his judgement of Jason contained some bias.

"It doesn't matter now. You already said you weren't going out with him again." He shrugged one shoulder. I rolled my eyes and glanced down at my wristwatch. It said it was fifteen minutes till one.

"Crap, I have to go." I hopped up and brushed the grass off my clothes. "Bye, Jared."

"Bye, Lizzie," he responded. I scrunched my nose at the nickname. "What?"

"We'll talk about it later," I told him and rushed off to work.

I hurried over to the coffee house, darting through the door right on time. I noticed the girl from last night was working the counter again today. I mentally crossed my fingers that she wasn't going to be my trainer, but as I scanned the room, I realized she was the only employee here. Her nametag read *Courtney*. I decided to put on my brightest face and hope I could win her over.

"Hi, my name's Beth. I was supposed to start today," I told her.

"Come to the back." Her voice was monotone. I wasn't sure if this was how she always was or if this was my own personal *welcome to the team* treatment. I nodded and did as she said. The back office was small. There was a manila folder with my name on it. My nametag lay on the desk next to the folder. "Fill out all that paperwork and then I'll show you a few things."

I mindlessly filled out all the forms and signed the bottom of various pages. My mind kept wandering back to Jared. It still bothered me how hard that memory had been to find. It was my *first kiss*, yet I hadn't thought about it since then. It should have been a memory I kept close by for daydreams. Why had it disappeared for so long? The more I followed the path, the more of the small moments I remembered. Images of young Jared flooded my mind. His blue eyes seemed bigger back then. His curl brushed across his forehead as he splashed in the creek. I was fearful of falling, but he held my hand.

"Are you finished?" Courtney asked, ripping me from my reverie.

"Oh, yeah. I'm done," I answered. I put on my nametag and followed her to the front. She gave me a quick tour and showed me how to work the different machines. I began to stock napkins into the containers. Courtney stared at me for a few moments before I asked, "What's up?"

"Nothing, it's just..." she trailed off. "I don't know. Nothing."

"What is it?"

"I just can't get over how much you look like her. I know that's probably not what you want to hear. Don't take this the wrong way, but it's kind of hard to be around you." She grabbed a broom and began to sweep.

"How could I possibly take that the wrong way?" I bit the inside of my cheek to hold in my irritation.

"I'm sorry. She was my best friend. Have you ever been close to someone who died?" she asked. My irritation melted away and sympathy replaced it.

"Yeah, actually, I have. I'm sorry. I know it's hard." I gave her a small smile.

"I think it would be easier if I knew who did it, you know? Like, why? Everyone loved her. She didn't have a single enemy. Who could possibly have had a reason to hurt her?" Her voice was tight with emotion.

"They'll catch the person," I assured. She nodded silently.

The rest of my shift was filled with coffee orders and scrubbing floors. I left close to nine. I was about halfway home when I felt eyes watching me. I twisted around expecting to see Jared, but the streets were deserted. Was Jared still following me around? No, it wouldn't make sense for him to hide now that I knew who he was. I was probably just imagining things.

As I stepped onto the porch, I noticed something sitting on the welcome mat. I squatted to pick it up. It appeared to be a couple of gifts. One was clearly a flower box and the other looked like a jewelry box. I carried the items into the house and set them on the kitchen table. I lifted the lid from the flower box and spotted a beautiful red flower that I couldn't identify. There was a card that had *Elizabeth* written on the front and inside it read: *Amaryllis is a symbol for splendid beauty*. There was no signature on the card, though. That's curious. Who would have sent this to me? I guess it could have been Jason, but he didn't seem deep enough for it. Jared, maybe? My heart fluttered at the possibility, but I quickly stomped it out. No, that would be crazy.

My eyes drifted to the jewelry box. Inside was a pair of red stud earrings that I recognized immediately as white gold. *These were expensive.* The red of the earrings matched the red of the flower. I didn't know who sent the gifts, but I would find out.

I opened my eyes the next morning to a brightly lit room. My brain registered that it was the sun and I was running late. I leapt from my bed and raced around the house like a chicken with its head cut off. I jogged to the school hoping to cut out some transit time. I managed to be on time, but just barely.

"Beth, the guidance counselor just called for you. He wants you to go to his office," Mr. Breacher announced before I even set my books down. I twirled back around and headed to the guidance counselor's office.

"Come in," I heard a male voice say from the other side of the door when I knocked.

"You wanted to see me?" I asked as I slid into the seat across from him. His nameplate told me he was Mr. Fisher.

"Yes, I did. I received a phone call from your mother this morning," he informed me.

"Oh." I knew I wouldn't like this.

"She's a real spitfire, that one." He smiled.

"Yes, that is certainly one word for it. So, what does she want you to do? Or should I ask, what does she want *you* to make *me* do?"

"Your mother feels like you aren't getting enough out of your senior year," he rambled.

"Just get to the point. What do I have to do?" The old me would have been horrified at how rude I sounded, but the new me hated when people danced around a subject.

"You have to join one club or activity," he announced.

"Seriously? Can she do that? I mean, she's not even here," I insisted.

"Until you're eighteen, she can make you do anything she wants," he stated.

"Fine, what are my choices?" I replied indignantly.

"Well, what are you good at? Your mom mentioned cheerleading." He flipped open a folder that had been laying on his desk.

"No. Not cheerleading. What about chess club? I know how to play chess," I offered. Technically, I knew how to play, but I wasn't all that good.

"Chess club is full. But it looks like they are needing someone for mathletes," he said. "Your records say you were in advanced placement math classes at your last school."

I frowned. "I don't think so. I'm not doing a ton more homework just to appease my mother."

"She made it a stipulation on your early release that you join something and mathletes is all that's left," he asserted. "Unless you want to take on full school days."

"Fine, whatever. Mathletes it is, then." I rolled my eyes. I couldn't believe Mom was micromanaging my life from five hundred miles away. Actually, I could. She'd always micromanaged my life. She had good intentions, but she never knew when to stop pushing.

"They meet in room 258 on Mondays and Wednesdays during lunch. I'll let them know you're coming." He dismissed me, and I shuffled from the room.

It'd been a long time since I was mad at Mom, but this pissed me off. She couldn't just call the school whenever I wouldn't do what she wanted. She was such a control freak. Anger poured through me. Without thinking, I swung my fist into the first locker I saw.

"Hey, what'd that locker ever do to you?" I heard Jared say from behind me.

"It existed." I gave him a side grin.

"Well, damn. I guess I better watch out," he joked.

I laughed. "Maybe you should." I began walking down the hall and he kept pace next to me.

"Trouble with your mom?"

I peeked at him from the corner of my eye. "How'd you know?"

"You always had a special expression reserved for when she made you angry." He shrugged.

"When was I ever mad at my mom?" I couldn't remember being angry with her.

"You were mad all the time." He laughed.

"You don't remember?" I shook my head and he continued. "She forced you to wear frilly pink dresses. You hated it. You would rebel by swimming in them or playing in the mud."

The memory slowly formed in my brain. Why was I having so much trouble remembering that summer? "Oh, yeah. I remember now. She was so pissed. Her face turned bright red." It made me realize that mom had always tried to force me into things I didn't want to do. It made me question every decision I had ever made. How much of it was what I actually wanted and how much of it was what *she* had wanted?

"So, what did she do this time?" he asked. It was interesting how we fell back into our groove, despite the ten-year gap.

"She's forcing me to join a group. Mathletes was the only thing with an opening." I groaned.

"Sounds like it could be fun," he encouraged.

"You did hear me say mathletes, right?" I frowned.

"I think you'll be surprised at how much you end up liking it. I know some of the guys and they're pretty cool," he insisted. I lifted a brow doubtfully. He laughed. "Okay, maybe cool isn't the right word for it. They're fun. Plus, they'll basically worship you. A pretty girl joining the mathletes is unheard of."

"I do enjoy being worshipped." I bit my lip as I pretended not to notice the part where he had called me pretty.

"That's the spirit. Now, go to class." He grinned.

"Wait, what about you? Why are you even out of class?" I asked. He gave me a wink and vanished down the hallway. "Whatever."

I didn't see Jared or Jason for the rest of the day. When I entered room 258, they appeared to have already started. There were five guys and four of them wore glasses. Did math somehow hinder a person's vision? Maybe it's true what they say: No one can have it all.

"Hi, I'm…" I began. One of the guys stood up abruptly. He had dark brown hair that was cut in a chili bowl style.

"Beth Michaels. Mr. Fisher said you were coming, but we didn't really believe him. Have a seat. My name's Jonathan. I'm the captain."

"For now. As soon as Vegas gets back, you're back to being co-captain," asserted another one of the guys. This one had blond hair gelled into short little spikes.

"*If* he comes back," Jonathan insisted. "I

can almost guarantee you, he hit it big and is living it up in the Bahamas."

"I'm sorry, who is Vegas?" I was confused. Vegas was a person?

"Oh, sorry. He was our captain, but he ran away last year. We've all got our theories on why," Jonathan explained.

"Why do you call him Vegas?" I had to ask.

"He got into some trouble for counting cards at a casino in Vegas. He was awesome at it, but he didn't lose enough, so he got caught. Which is why I think he improved his game and went back," Jonathan told me.

"No, he swore he was done with all that," argued the blond one.

"And you think he was able to give up that much money? I wouldn't," Jonathan asserted.

"Vegas isn't you." Blondie glared at Jonathan.

"Sorry, I didn't mean to cause a fight." I slid into the nearest seat.

"Don't worry about it. Craig and Jonathan fight all the time. Everyone just misses Vegas. It hasn't been the same since he left," said a guy with thin rimmed glasses and shaggy brown hair. "I'm Kent, by the way."

"Nice to meet you," I responded.

"And that's Chris and that's Mario." Kent pointed at the other two guys who were sitting quietly. They nodded in acknowledgement. I smiled in response.

"Okay, let's do some math," Jonathan exclaimed.

CHAPTER FOUR

SECRETS FORGOTTEN

The water in the creek sparkles almost magically. The sun shines down, but it isn't hot by any means. It's the perfect temperature. I want to swim. I glance around. I am alone. I tug off my clothes until I'm only in my bra and underwear. I race to the edge of the creek and dip my toe in. It is also the perfect temperature. I step into the water. The creek isn't deep, maybe four feet. It comes up to the bottom edge of my bra.

"You always were a little water sprite," Jared teases from the edge of the water. He leans down to speak to me. I take advantage of the moment and tug him into the creek. When his head resurfaces, he is laughing. He splashes me in revenge. When we are both out of breath, we pause. His eyes soak me in and something fills them. They look hungry. My heart pounds fast under his gaze. His wet shirt clings to his chest muscles, revealing his athletic tone.

He inches closer to me. I don't move, not sure what I want. No, that's not true. I know what I want. I just don't know if I want to want it. I'm not making any sense. It's too late now. He wraps his arms around my waist. I press into his chest, feeling his strong arms encircle me. His lips are reticent as they brush across my forehead. I lift my face to stare him straight in the eye.

"What's the matter?" I ask him. Guilt flashes across his face.

"Is this what you want?" he asks as he runs his hand along the side of my face. His thumb traces my bottom lip causing heat to boil me from within.

"Yes," I answer.

His eyes search my face. I lift myself onto my tiptoes and place my lips to his. It is soft at first. He cups my face with his hands. I feel the urge to go deeper. My arms creep around him and squeeze him closer. His lips press into mine with an urgency that soon spreads through me. After a moment, he pulls away.

"I wish this was real," he murmurs under his breath.

"What do you mean?" I am confused. He doesn't answer me. Instead, he wraps my hand into his and helps me out of the stream.

"Let's dance like we used to. Do you remember?" he asks me. I laugh as he tugs me closer to him. He twirls us around in a circle.

"Why is it I only remember things after you tell me about them?" I ask him curiously.

"I think your mind wanted to forget some things from that summer. Maybe it got carried away." His words make little sense to me. Why would my mind wish to forget things? That was silly. *"I like seeing you like this,"* he whispers near my ear.

"Like what?" I ask as he twirls us again.

"Happy." He smiles down at me and I smile back.

"I'm sorry my brain made me forget you." I bite my lip.

"It was protecting you. I can't be mad at that." He tucks a strand of my hair behind my ear. We twist again and this time he dips me.

"Protecting me from what?" I ask as I cock my head to the side, staring up at him.

"Now, why would you want to dig up painful memories?" He avoids the question with his own question.

"I deserve to know the truth," I assert. He lifts me up and tugs me close to him.

"You should trust yourself. If you could handle the memory, you would remember," he contends. Anger cuts through the euphoric feeling I was experiencing.

"You know!" I accuse. *"You know and you won't tell me."* I wriggle out of his embrace and cross my arms over my chest.

"You won't want to know," he maintains.

"How will I know if you do not tell me?" I frown.

"If I told you, you would hate me for doing so," he

insists.

I woke with a start. That was a strange dream. There was something very realistic about it. I shuddered as I glanced around the dark room. An eerie feeling crawled across my skin. *Someone was in here.* I darted to my light switch and flicked it on. My breathing was heavy as my eyes searched the room. It was empty, but I couldn't brush off the feeling that someone *had* been in here. *I'm just tired*, I told myself. My heart still pounded heavily in my chest.

My eyes fell back to my bed where a doll lay near my pillow. Unsure of how it got into my bed, I picked it up to examine it closer. It had dark brown hair with rosy cheeks and tiny, dark eyes. I smoothed out its pale, yellow dress. It was one of the china dolls from my grandmother's collection. It had always been my favorite. I remembered playing with it every time I came to visit. I glanced over to the shelf on the wall that held the rest of the dolls. The spot where this one went was now empty. Maybe I got up in the middle of the night and grabbed it for whatever reason. I carefully placed the doll back in its designated spot on the shelf.

I grabbed a throw blanket and a pillow and sauntered down the stairs. I still felt uneasy in the room after the way I woke up and didn't care to be in there. I instantly noticed that the front door was unlocked and the eerie feeling returned. I quickly locked the deadbolt and glanced out the window. There was nothing. I flopped onto the couch and turned the television on. I spent the next hour watching reruns before I finally dozed off again.

I woke early the next morning before the sun was up. I glanced up at the television. It remained on the same channel I had fallen asleep to, but now it aired the morning news. I turned up the volume as I gathered my bedding from the couch.

"Authorities in Idaho have issued an Amber Alert for seventeen-year-old Marlene Dougherty. Police say she was last seen in Nampa leaving her job at the Onetrip gas station on Meacham Street late Sunday night. Police are asking for any information the public may have on Marlene's whereabouts," a newscaster reported as I half-listened. I glanced up at the screen and gasped in shock. The girl that was displayed looked strikingly similar to me. Her nose was slightly longer and her mouth a little smaller, but she could definitely play my stunt double in a movie.

My eyes darted to the front door. Last

night's fear crept back into my mind. I had felt someone in my room. My instinct told me someone had been watching me sleep. My rational side chimed in. It was only a dream. And the front door was left unlocked by a careless Aunt Meredith. That made sense and I clung to the logical explanation – the *safe* explanation.

I forced it from my mind. I felt a twitch in my leg. My muscles yearned for me to exercise. I hadn't worked out since the accident. I had gotten the okay from my doctor weeks ago but never got around to picking my routine back up. My body seemed to be ordering me to jump back into it today. I had discovered a great jogging route when I explored the town on Sunday.

After throwing on some workout clothes and doing a few stretches, I started my jog along the path that led around the park. The morning temperature wasn't as hot as the afternoon but it was humid. Sweat trickled down my forehead nearly instantly. Despite the thickness to the air, the jog felt amazing. It was as if I were reconnecting with a small part of my old self.

"I wondered how long it would take you to find this place," I heard Jason's breathy voice say from beside me. He was wearing a black muscle tee with a pair of black shorts with white lines on the sides. He was sweaty and appeared to have been jogging for a while.

"Hi," I greeted a little higher than normal, not responding to his comment.

Jason's arrogance was his worst feature. He was presumptuous. I didn't like that he thought he knew me or could predict what I'd do when we'd only just met. He smiled showing off his dimples. I could admire how attractive he was, though. And he had his good moments, the few that were slightly humble. I stayed my course as Jason jogged next to me.

"Are you angry with me for going to the party?" he asked, catching my unintentional inflection.

"Nope," I answered honestly.

"Alright, then." He switched subjects. "So, did you get the job at the coffee house?"

"Yeah, I started on Sunday," I told him.

"How do you like it?"

"So far, so good," I replied. We were silent, apart from our heavy breathing, for a moment after that.

"Hey, I have an idea. You want to race?" He grinned over at me.

A determined smile spread over my face. "You're on."

"To the edge of the park. Let's say, first one to that tree wins." He pointed. I nodded. "Ready? Set, go!" We rushed from our standing positions in pursuit of the tree. I knew he'd be fast since he was a football player, but I also knew I'd be faster. My light weight and slender muscles gave me the upper hand. Of course, he wasn't bowing out, by any means. We were neck to neck up until the last moment. I pushed harder and was the first to place my hand on the tree.

"I win," I yelled with a giggle.

"Just barely!" He laughed as he grabbed me around the waist. He spun me around and my foot twisted with his. We fell to the ground in a heap. Somehow, I ended up underneath him. He held himself up with his elbows on either side of me. "You tripped me," he whispered.

"More like you dropped me," I teased. Well, it seemed we had found our common ground. We were both extremely competitive.

His proximity suddenly reminded me of the earrings. "Do you like my earrings?" I said in a hinting tone. He laughed at the randomness of the question, considering we had just toppled to the ground.

"Anything would look beautiful on you," he whispered. The lack of recognition in his tone told me he wasn't the one to leave me the gifts.

His face was inches from mine as he smiled down at me. Intensity filled his eyes and I knew he was going to kiss me. I was almost inclined to let him, but then Jared's face flashed in my mind. Suddenly, my dream last night came to the forefront of my brain. There had to be a reason I was dreaming of kissing Jared. Did I have feelings for him? I couldn't answer that. However, I felt I shouldn't allow more to happen with Jason until I knew. I shifted my face so that his kiss landed on my cheek. His eyes opened in surprise.

"I should probably go shower before school," I told him. Confusion covered his face, but he moved off me. "I'll see you later." I waved goodbye and headed home.

I avoided Jason the whole day at school. He might have been avoiding me, too, but there was no way to tell. I had no work after school that day, so I decided I'd glance through the packet the mathletes had given me the day before. The sky was clear and sunny as I strolled home. The thought of being inside was not appealing, so I headed to the creek instead. I preferred to study outside. Actually, I preferred doing anything outside when the weather was nice.

I leaned back against the tree near the creek

and lifted the packet to read. The first section seemed easy enough. Once I made it through the second section without any hiccups, I felt more confident. But then the third section came. I stared at the problems with an expression I'm sure matched the one I had when attempting to read a German novel.

"What is that?" Jared appeared next to me. His sudden presence startled me.

"My mathlete packet," I grumbled.

"Don't sound too excited." Jared laughed.

"Why did I let you convince me this would be anything other than torture? I don't even know what anything on this page is." I gestured at the packet in frustration.

Jared laughed at my angry outburst. I glared at him, but it didn't alter his smile one bit. However, he did begin to explain what the math problems were asking. It turned out, I *did* know how to work the problem, and I just let the question throw me off course.

"Why do they have to trick us? Why can't they just be straightforward with what they are asking?" I rolled my eyes at the page.

"It's not about tricking you. It's teaching you to think critically," he insisted. I raised one skeptical brow at him. He laughed, causing me to crack a smile.

"Well, since *you're* so good at all this, why don't *you* join the mathletes?"

"Then you wouldn't have a club to be a member of," he pointed out. "Besides, I have far more important things to do with my time," he joked.

"Like stalk me?" I teased.

"Oh, you think you're the only girl I stalk? You're quite full of yourself, aren't you?" His grin grew until it reached his eyes making his already handsome face even more attractive.

"Don't make up other girls just to make me jealous. It won't work," I declared.

"No? Not even a little?" His eyes lowered to my lips, causing my heart to beat faster.

"Well, maybe a little," I admitted.

His eyes remained locked on my lips as I leaned in to kiss him. He jerked back in surprise. Shock and embarrassment flooded me. I didn't understand his reaction. Had I read the signals wrong?

"I'll let you get back to work." He hurried off without an explanation.

What was that about? Did he have a girl-friend, maybe? As sexy as he was, I'm sure he did. It was naive for me to assume he was single. Plus, he didn't say anything about the earrings, which had been in his clear view. If they weren't from Jared or Jason, then who were they from? Ugh, I was more disappointed that Jared had not given them to me than I thought I would've been.

Jared refused to leave my mind. Even my dreams had him, yet again. We were back at the creek sitting under the tree. We held hands and spoke of nothing in particular. When I awoke, I instantly missed his presence, which was ridiculous. It was a dream.

Once I arrived at school, I was surprised to see a girl I recognized as the head cheerleader standing at my locker. She appeared to be Hispanic and she was drop-dead gorgeous. She had long, dark hair with big brown eyes. Her lips were full and covered in red lipstick.

"Hi, I'm Gloria." She offered her hand to me. I slowly took it, unsure of why she was introducing herself to me.

"Beth," I responded.

"Oh, I know!" Her voice was as cheerful as her uniform. "A little birdy told me you were a cheerleader at your last school."

Panic seized me. What else did this little birdy tell her about my last school? "Yeah," I said slowly.

"Well, we have a position open. It's yours if you want it," she offered.

"You don't even know if I'm any good." I frowned.

"I have a good sense about these things." Her grin filled up the entire bottom half of her face.

"Well, regardless, I'm not interested," I replied. Her grin fell at my words.

"Are you sure? This is a great opportunity. We rarely have any openings," she persuaded.

"That's okay. Really," I asserted.

"I see." Her voice no longer held any cheer. Something shifted in her entire demeanor. "Well, I was hoping to do this with a little more civility, but I guess you leave me no choice."

"What are you talking about?" I narrowed my eyes.

"Jason is taken. Stay away from him," she ordered.

My expression turned to knowing as realization hit me.

"You were trying to manipulate me by getting me on the squad." I shook my head in annoyance.

"Just stay away from him." She glared at me with such intensity, I thought my skin might burn under the weight of it.

"I don't intimidate easily. I'll hang out with who I want, when I want, and *you* will not factor into any of it," I assured her.

"You just made yourself a new enemy." She glanced over to a group of cheerleaders that watched our encounter. "Make that *enemies*."

I bit my tongue in an attempt to hold back any more commentary. *This was the opposite of what I had wanted.* I had planned to *not* get involved in any drama. Yet, here I was, the new target of the head cheerleader. But the thought of her barking orders at me like she ruled the school just pissed me off. If I wanted to date Jason, then I would freaking date Jason. The problem was, I wasn't actually *sure* what I wanted.

I was fuming for all of first period, but by the time lunch rolled around, I had cooled off. I made my way to room 258 to meet with the mathletes. I handed my packet to Jonathan who took it with a befuddled expression. He flipped through it and raised his eyebrows in astonishment.

"You finished this whole thing in two days?" His voice was in awe.

"Actually, I did it yesterday. I thought you wanted it done by today." I didn't understand his reaction.

"I meant next Wednesday, not this Wednesday. This should have taken you much longer to finish." Jonathan shifted so that the other team members could see.

"I mean, I hit a couple of snags, but it wasn't that hard. My friend helped me with some of it," I admitted.

"Does this friend go to school here?" Jonathan asked.

"Yeah, he does," I replied.

"Well, tell him if he wants to be on the mathletes, we can kick Craig out," Jonathan offered.

"Uh, excuse me? You don't have that power." Craig scowled over at Jonathan.

"I don't think he's interested in joining anyway," I announced.

"Well, even so, you're a great addition. Maybe we can actually win some tournaments. It's been a terrible year without Vegas," Jonathan said. "You're our new secret weapon."

I smiled at the compliment. Maybe, Jared was right. I think I might just like the mathletes, after all.

CHAPTER FIVE

SECRETS DREAMS

Work that day *sucked*. Gloria's threats were not empty ones. She spent hours at the coffee house with Kathy and Stephanie. Their lattes were too sweet, then not sweet enough. Their lattes were too creamy, then not creamy enough. When they finally accepted their drinks, they each made a point of placing a single penny into the tip jar. I took deep breaths in the break room to keep from jumping over the counter and pouring coffee over each one of their heads.

Let it go, I told myself. *It's not worth it.* But wasn't it? I sighed. *No.* I liked my job. So, I put up with the jabs, complaints, and snickering for the next couple of hours before they finally left. I just prayed they'd get bored and not come back again.

After the coffee shop closed and I cleaned my area, I left through the back exit in case the cheerleaders stuck around to harass me some more. Jared stepped around the corner, startling me.

"What are you doing out here?" I asked.

"Waiting for you to get off." He shrugged. "Mind if I walk you home?"

"I can't control where you walk," I teased.

"True." He strolled beside me at an easy pace. "So, what did you do to piss off the Rat Pack?"

"You saw all that?" I asked. He nodded. I rolled my eyes as I continued, "Apparently, Jason is Gloria's property."

"Oh." The single word held meaning, but I couldn't decipher what that was.

"Yeah, I guess she heard I went on a date with him, so now I'm an enemy of the state. Well, an enemy of the squad, anyway." I frowned.

"What are you going to do about it?" He gave me a sidelong glance.

"Nothing. If I retaliate, it'll only start a war and I just don't have the energy for that." I shrugged.

"That's a mature attitude." He winked. "But a good catfight would have been fun to watch."

A thought struck me and suspicion clouded my thoughts. I didn't remember seeing him in the coffee house today. So, how did he know what

Gloria, Kathy, and Stephanie were doing? Maybe, he *had* been there and I was too distracted with the cheerleaders to notice. I brushed off my initial suspicion.

"Well, let's see how the year goes. You may get that catfight, yet." I smiled.

"So, why didn't you just tell her you're not dating Jason?" His eyes studied my face.

"Because I don't have to explain myself to her. She tried to intimidate me into doing what she wants. That's not going to happen," I asserted.

"So, then, you *are* going to date Jason?" His tone sounded puzzled.

"Well, no, but she doesn't have the right to tell me I *can't*." I could tell Jared did *not* get the way girls thought because he just shook his head in exasperation.

"Whatever you say." He laughed. We came to a stop in front of my house. "Well, goodnight." He paused. His eyes fell back to my mouth, and I got the sense that he wanted to kiss me. But something stopped him. Maybe, I was right and he had a girlfriend.

"Goodnight," I muttered and entered the house.

I fell asleep quickly once I lay in bed and I

found myself back in dream world with Jared.

Jared lays under the tree as I walk up to him. He gazes up at me with a lazy smile on his face. He gestures for me to join him, so I crawl next to his side. He wraps his arm around my waist and I lay against his chest.

"I'm sorry I didn't let you kiss me. Just know that I wanted to," he whispers.

"I don't understand." If he wanted to, then why didn't he?

"I know. I'm sorry." His hand brushes lightly over my arm, leaving small tingles in its wake. I cuddle close to him and his arm tightens around me. His lips graze the top of my head and he mumbles something in a language I don't understand.

"What was that?" I ask in a soft voice.

"Italian," he answers.

"What did you say?" I shift so I can see his face. His eyes study mine.

"I said, you are beautiful." A blush burns at my cheeks, but I don't break our eye contact. Instead, I lift myself so that I am within inches of his face.

"Why didn't you kiss me?" I want to know his answer.

"Do you remember our first kiss?" he asks without answering my question.

"Yes, I ran home afterwards." I smile.

"I'm scared that if I tell you the truth, then you'll

run again," he admits.

"You can tell me anything. I promise I won't run,"
I swear.

"Same to you," he says.

"What do you mean?" I bite my lip as I glance
away from his face.

He draws my face back to him. "What happened in
Oregon? Why'd you move here?"

I bite the inside of my cheek in contemplation. I
have been needing to talk about it and dream Jared was
probably the safest person to do so with. "Everyone hates
me there."

"What? Why?" His voice sounds alarmed.

"I did something bad." My voice cracks and I'm
suddenly fearful of what Jared might think of me when I
tell him the truth. Will he hate me, too?

His fingers gently hold my chin. "I said I wouldn't
run. Tell me what happened."

I take a deep breath and tell him the whole story,
every last gritty detail. Soon, tears are falling down my face
and I can't seem to hold them back. His fingers wipe them
away before he tugs me against his chest.

"Everyone makes mistakes. I promise that this one
does not make you a bad person." He rubs my back in a
reassuring manner. A tiny memory peeks its head out of
the shadows.

"I just remembered something else from when we

were kids," I announce.

"What is it?" he asks, his voice masking an unknown emotion.

"I remember crying on your shoulder. I don't remember why, though. I think I might have been hurt. Do you remember?" I ask him.

"You cried so often, I couldn't possibly know to which time you are referring," he teases.

"I did not!" I laugh. I know I cried a lot as a little girl, but this memory seems different. I was terrified and I was... bleeding? It slowly comes back to me in small increments like puzzle pieces falling into place. I was bleeding from my shoulder. I glance down at my scar. "It was the day I got this." I move my strap over so he sees my scar. He traces a finger over the pink skin. My body shivers in response. "I don't remember how it happened though. Did I fall or something?" I ask him.

"Or something," he answers.

He bends down and places his lips to my scar and all thoughts of the memory flee my brain. He kisses along my neck. Breathing becomes difficult as he slowly makes his way to my lips. He places a small kiss on either side of my mouth before pausing. The moment is intense as he stares down at me with hungry eyes.

"You really are beautiful," he murmurs.

Something explodes in my chest at his words and I can no longer contain my desire. I slide my hand through his hair and guide his lips to mine. He gives no resistance as our mouths meet. His lips move easily with mine as I crawl onto his lap. His arms wrap around my waist as I am pulled tighter against his body. I never want this moment to end. His lips are light as he presses them along my jawline.

He seems to gather control over himself and pulls back. "I'm sorry."

"Why do you always apologize?" I am puzzled by his reaction.

"I shouldn't be here. I have no right," he says, confusing me further.

"Down by the creek?" I ask.

Although we are no longer kissing, I am still on his lap and he still has his arms around me.

"No, in your dream. I shouldn't be here, kissing you like this. It's not right. It's just..." he trails off.

I don't understand why he thinks he shouldn't be here. It's my dream. I'm the one who put him here.

"It's just what?" I study his face as his eyes glance over to the side.

"I've thought about you so often since we were kids. I never thought I'd actually see you again. It would be my luck that you come back after it's too late." He leans his head back against the tree. His eyes are shut and frustration covers every inch of him.

"Do you have a girlfriend?" I ask curiously. He

lifts his eyelids only enough to look at me through slits.

"No, I wish that were the problem. I would break up with her in an instant for you," he declares. Warmth spreads through me.

"Then, whatever the problem is, it doesn't belong in this place. It's a real-world problem. Real-world problems do not exist in my dream. That's a new rule." I grin down at him. His eyes open as he lets out a laugh.

"Well, just remember you said that." He tugs me down for another kiss.

My alarm beeped loudly from my bedside table. I swatted at it until it finally stopped. I stared up at the ceiling, unable to get my dream out of my head. These dreams of Jared were starting to get out of hand. I felt like an obsessed freak. Who dreams about a guy every single night? And how is it I'm able to remember every detail so clearly? Usually, my dreams were fuzzier than analog television.

As I tossed my covers aside, I heard a thump as something fell from the bed. I leaned over to see what it was. My stomach clenched when I saw the dark-haired china doll. Fear planted from countless horror movies I'd seen began to grow inside me. This was really starting to creep me out. I hurried over to my closet and placed the doll on the shelf. I felt better now that it was no longer in my view.

I started my jog early that morning in hopes of getting a longer workout. The more often I worked out, the more I needed to. I considered for a moment joining the track team, but it interfered with mathletes so I decided against it. Mathletes was turning out to be more fun than I expected. Who knew? Well, Jared knew. For someone who hadn't been around me in ten years, he sure did know a lot about me. I guess sometimes when you meet certain people, they just *got* you. They got who you are and what you're about without having to say anything.

Ugh, this crush on Jared was starting to get annoying. He obviously didn't like me like that or he wouldn't have pulled away when I tried to kiss him. What was it he had told me in my dream? That he had wanted to? He didn't really explain why he hadn't kissed me though. Not that it made a difference. It was just a dream, but you would think my brain would have come up with *something* to ease the rejection.

I thought back to that first dream I had of Jared. The one where we had been swimming. Something Jared said had been playing over in my mind ever since. He had said that my brain forgot that summer for a reason. Was that true? Had something happened that was so awful my brain made me forget everything? I glanced down at my scar as I felt a small heat pulse through it. Why couldn't I remember how I got it? Maybe my mind was leading me to the answer through my dreams. Jared may know something about it. I made a mental note to ask him later.

"Good morning." Jason jogged up next to me. This seemed to be our new routine, which I didn't altogether mind.

"Good morning," I said in a chipper voice.

"Well, someone's cheerful today." Jason grinned, showing off his dimples. "Does it have anything to do with the video of Gloria that's going around the school?"

"What video?" I started jogging in place as Jason tugged out his cell phone.

"I thought you might've been the one to send it out," he admitted.

"I don't have a computer or cell phone, so it definitely wasn't me," I told him.

Curiosity overwhelmed me as he hit play on the video. I leaned closer to him to get a better view of the screen. It appeared to be some sort of video diary that Gloria had recorded on her laptop. She was speaking to the webcam and said a date that was only a few weeks ago.

"Okay, diary. This is the most embarrassing thing that has ever happened to me. Last night, I had a sex dream about…" She glanced away from the camera in faux drama, as if the name were so terrible, she couldn't even bring herself to speak it. "Jonathan Weber. The truly awful thing is… it wasn't the first one. I've had them so often that I sometimes look at him in school and wonder what it would be like in real life. Uh, this is mortifying. I shouldn't even be recording this. I'm deleting this video, right now." The video ended there.

"Well, Jonathan will be thrilled when he sees this," I commented as I pictured the mathletes' captain doing his little happy dance.

"*Everyone's* seen this video," Jason stated. "Gloria will be on a rampage today. Be prepared because I'm sure she's going to blame you."

"But I didn't even know about the stupid video." I rolled my eyes.

"Gloria tends to believe what she wants to," Jason asserted. "Like the fact that she thinks we're still an item, which we are not. She just can't let things go."

"Yeah, I kind of got that when she spent the entire day at my job making me miserable." I threw my left arm across my chest to stretch out the muscles.

"I'm sorry. If there was something I could do to make it better, I would. As it is, if I ask her to back off, it'll only make it worse for you." He gave me an apologetic smile.

"Thanks, but I can fight my own battles. I've dealt with snotty cheerleaders all of high school," I assured.

"Oh, I have no doubt you can handle yourself." He grabbed my hand and tugged me over to him. His smoky blue eyes stared down at me. Something churned in the back of my mind like it wanted to come forward, but it couldn't. Jason placed his hands on my shoulders as he shifted me into a kiss. As his lips brushed across mine, I felt his thumbs play with the straps of my tank top. I jolted when his thumb found my scar. Being self-conscious of it for so long, I had become hyper aware of anyone touching it. His expression became quizzical. "Did I hurt you?"

"No, you didn't." I stepped back and gave him a grin. "Want to race?" I challenged.

CHAPTER SIX

SECRET ENEMIES

Jason was right. Gloria stormed through the hall screaming at anyone who dared bring up the video. As hard as I tried to avoid her, she managed to catch me in the girls' bathroom after second period. I pretended not to notice as Gloria, Kathy, and Stephanie burst through the door. I grabbed a paper towel to dry my freshly washed hands.

"You seriously have a death wish," Gloria accused. "I know you were the one to hack into my laptop and steal that video."

"Yeah, I don't even know how to do that," I contended.

"Then, you had one of your geeky mathlete friends do it. Either way, I know you were behind it," she barked.

I rolled my eyes and attempted to push past her to leave. She shoved me backward.

"Let me through or I'll break that dainty,

little nose of yours," I threatened.

"Uh!" She squeaked, instinctively placing her hand over her nose. I took the moment to dart around her and exit the bathroom. If only everyone realized how easy it was to take down a cheerleader. Just threaten their faces.

I knew that wouldn't be the last of things, but I was still determined to be the bigger person and not get sucked into their pettiness. They weren't making it easy, though. After third period, as I strolled toward my locker, someone's leg appeared in front of my feet and I tumbled to the ground. I spotted Gloria, Kathy, and Stephanie giggling as they departed the scene of the crime. I rolled my eyes and began to gather my now scattered books.

"Hey, let me help you with that," I heard a female voice say. I was shocked when I glanced up to see a girl in a cheerleading uniform. She bent down and helped me gather my things.

"Thanks," I muttered.

"No problem." She glanced over her shoulder at Gloria who was glaring daggers at us. "And don't worry about Gloria. Someone else will cross her soon enough and she'll move on to her next victim."

"Good to know." I straightened out some

of my papers that had gotten crinkled in the fall.

"I'm Cindy, by the way." The girl smiled. She had strawberry blonde hair that appeared to be naturally curly.

"I'm Beth, but I'm sure you knew that." I smiled back at her.

"Oh, yeah. I've heard plenty, but I'm sure none of it's true." She tried for a reassuring smile, but my thoughts were on my past. If anyone knew, surely I'd have heard about it. My paranoia was getting the better of me.

"I'm sure," I responded lightly. "Well, thanks, again, for helping me."

Cindy was apparently in my next class. I guess I never paid much attention. Today, she sat next to me and proceeded to chitchat with me as if we were longtime friends. She seemed like one of those girls who could get along with anyone. That used to be me at my old school. I never cared about whether a person was popular or not. I was nice to you if you were nice to me. I decided that should still be my motto and not let the fact that Cindy was a cheerleader affect the way I treated her. I smiled as she rambled on about a party that was being held tomorrow night in the cemetery.

"You should come," she asserted.

"No, thanks. Parties aren't really my thing," I told her.

"Come *on*. What else could you possibly be doing on a Friday night that'll be more fun?" she insisted.

"One word. Netflix," I contended.

"Seriously?" She arched a perfectly shaped brow. "This is our *senior year*. Our last chance to be as crazy as we want and only be prosecuted as minors." She winked.

I laughed. "Well, when you put it that way." I debated her offer. What could one party hurt? As long as I didn't drink, then where was the harm? "Sure. Why not?"

"Yay!" She squealed. She told me to meet her there at nine.

The rest of the day, Gloria stayed out of my way. I wasn't sure if it was because of my threat to break her face or if she was planning something. My gut told me it was the latter. There was little I could do about her pending undeserved retaliation, so I tried not to think about it. Work was slow, so Susan had us deep cleaning everything. When I left, I walked out the back door to see Jared waiting to walk me home again.

"Hey." I smiled, genuinely happy to see him. Warmth stole over me when he returned the smile with just as much sincerity.

"How was work?" he asked, making small talk.

"Fine. How was your... whatever it is you do all day?" I instantly realized I had no clue what that was.

"It was fine." He laughed.

"Alrighty then," I said when he didn't divulge any details. "Did you see that video of Gloria?"

"Yep." He grinned with a hint of mischief.

"What's with that expression? Did you have something to do with it?" I eyed him suspiciously.

"I have no idea what you're talking about." His grin grew.

"I can't believe you did that." I laughed.

"I admit to nothing." He winked.

I shook my head in amusement. "Whatever." I paused before asking, "Are you going to the party at the cemetery tomorrow night?"

"No, why? Are you?" His dark eyebrows were high as he turned towards me.

"Yeah, I think so."

"Are you sure that's a good idea?"

"What do you mean?" I gave him a peering expression.

"I just thought you wouldn't want to after..." he trailed off.

"After what?" I turned on him. My stomach dropped. Maybe my paranoia had something to it. He seemed to be hinting at the accident. But how did he know? And who else knew?

"Nothing." He brushed off the question as we came to a stop at my door. "Have fun at the party."

"Thanks. I will." I bit my lip to keep from bringing up his comment. If he didn't know, then my paranoia would tell him if I couldn't rein it in. I tugged out my key to unlock the door.

"Hey, Lizzie," he said quietly. I thought about correcting him, but I found that I kind of liked it when he called me Lizzie.

"Yeah?" I asked as I focused on inserting the key.

"Be careful," he warned.

"Why do I need...?" I turned around to see that Jared was gone. I suddenly remembered I had planned to ask about my scar. I kicked myself for forgetting. With the distraction of Jared, I didn't notice that someone had left a couple more gifts on my doorstep, and I accidently bumped them with my foot. It was the same this time. There was a flower box and a jewelry box. I opened the flower box first again. This time, I recognized the flower as a white lily. The card read: *Calla Lily represents purity and innocence.* Again, there was no signature. I reread the card as needles prickled my skin. The first flower was sweet, but this one was bizarre. Purity and innocence? I tossed the strange card aside and opened the jewelry box. Inside was a white diamond cluster pendant necklace. I had seen this one at the mall. It cost a pretty penny.

I bit my lip. It was gorgeous. As creepy as the message that came with it was, it wasn't as if I could return the gift. I had no clue who sent it. It didn't take much to convince myself to keep it. I laced it around my neck and clasped the chain. The pendant fell just below my shirt. I threw out the flower and card not wanting my aunt to come across it.

I awoke the next morning cuddled next to something small. I opened my eyes sleepily and peered at a porcelain face gazing back at me. I let out a scream and nearly flung the doll against the hard wall. Luckily, it landed on my chair without breaking. As much as the doll was freaking me out, I didn't want to break something that my grandmother had cherished.

My heart beat violently in my chest as I stared at the inanimate object. *That's what it is, an inanimate object,* I reminded myself. My heart did not believe me, for it continued its furious beating.

After watching the doll for more than five minutes and it lying motionless the entire time, – duh! it's a doll – I tiptoed over to it. I felt ridiculous in my actions, but I couldn't help it. I put that doll up in my closet. How the hell did it get into my bed? This time, I was moving it to the attic. There was no way I could sleepwalk up there.

After I successfully placed the doll upstairs in the attic, I decided to do some yoga instead of my morning jog to calm my nerves. Besides, just because I wasn't a cheerleader anymore didn't mean I had to lose my flexibility. At school, Cindy reminded me about the party. I think she was concerned I was going to back out. Which I had considered, but in the end, I kept to my decision of going but not drinking.

As promised, Cindy was waiting for me at the gate when I arrived at the cemetery. She was wearing a tight miniskirt with a bright pink spaghetti strap. The night was a little chilly so I'd opted to wear jeans and a light blue top.

"You look cute," Cindy complimented. "Looking forward to seeing anyone in particular?"

"Not really." I gave her a sidelong glance.

"It's okay if you like Jason." She laughed. "I don't care one way or the other. Gloria is the one with the crazy obsession."

"I don't know if I like Jason," I admitted.

"Well, you might want to figure it out soon because he's headed our way." She gestured her head to the right. My eyes trailed off in the direction she referred to and spotted Jason. He must have just arrived, as well.

"Hey," he called over. Once he reached us, he slid his hand into mine. "I missed you on my jog this morning." His tone sounded disappointed.

"Oh, yeah, I wanted to mix it up some. I did a little yoga instead," I explained.

"So, you're not avoiding me?" He tugged me closer to him. Part of me felt excited by the attention he was giving me, but part of me wished it were Jared that was showing me such affection.

"No, I promise." I smiled.

"Good." He wrapped his arm around my shoulders and led me into the cemetery. People were crowded around in groups. A keg was set up near a large tombstone with cups and other drinks in metal buckets of ice. "Want a beer?"

"No thanks. I'm not drinking tonight," I told him.

"I'll see if I can find us something nonalcoholic," Cindy chimed in. She disappeared toward the drink area. Jason's phone let out a small beep, and he glanced at the screen.

"Jimmy just brought another keg. He needs help carrying it. I'll be right back." He gave me a quick kiss on the cheek before I could respond. Just as he vanished, Cindy reappeared holding two red solo cups. She handed me one and I instantly sniffed it.

"No alcohol, I promise." She smiled. I took a sip and it tasted of sweet punch. No sharp bite of alcohol whatsoever, so I took a bigger gulp. I suddenly felt parched. I quickly finished off the punch, and I wanted more.

I took a small step toward the drinks but felt a wave of dizziness settle over me. Something wasn't right. I couldn't hold a train of thought. My vision swam as my body became foreign to me. Fear gripped me but was soon replaced by a euphoric feeling. Someone turned the music up and I became lost in the moment. All I wanted to do was dance.

More time must have gone by than I had thought because Jason was making his way back over to me. It didn't feel like enough time had passed for him to have helped carry a keg from the street to where it sat now, but it must have been. Once he stepped within arm's reach, I grabbed him and began dancing.

He laughed. "Whoa, I thought you weren't drinking tonight."

"I'm not." I giggled.

I wrapped my arms around his shoulders as he slipped his around my waist. Our bodies pressed together as the music played on. He whispered something in my ear, but my mind couldn't follow the stream of words. Everything around us spun or maybe we were the ones spinning. I could not tell.

"Are you feeling alright?" he asked when I lost my balance for no particular reason. "Did you take something?" I thought I could hear concern in his voice, but I couldn't focus on anything for longer than a second.

"No." I shook my head, but it only made the dizziness worse. Nothing would stay still. Even Jason's face was rotating in an unnatural way. I gripped his arm for support as I became unsteady on my feet.

"You don't look so good. I'm taking you home," Jason declared. He moved me over to the nearest tree. "Here, hold on to this while I find Jimmy. He has the keys to my jeep." I nodded, unable to do anything else. I leaned against the tree as Jason disappeared to hunt down Jimmy.

My legs wobbled as my head became light. My vision spotted with black dots as I felt myself losing consciousness. My grip on the tree loosened as I fell to the ground. I felt hands grip under my shoulders and I could tell I was being dragged somewhere. My vision blurred in and out. I could only make out a dark figure looming over me. I didn't know who it was or where they were taking me. I couldn't hold back the draw any longer and soon fell into an unconscious state.

"Lizzie! You have to wake up."

"Jared?"

I thought sleeping would make the woozy feeling better, but it didn't. Everything is spinning here, too. I can't find Jared amongst the twisting chaos.

"Lizzie! Listen to me. You have to wake up. Now!" Jared sounds frantic which causes my heart to slam against my ribs.

"I can't. The spinning... it's too much. I can't concentrate," I cry.

"Just look at me. Look at my face." Jared's face appears right next to mine. He places both hands on my shoulders and locks my gaze with his. "Just focus on my

eyes, Lizzie. You can do this. You have to do this."

I woke up, barely conscious, but it was enough to see I was in trouble. My eyes darted around, but I could no longer see people. I could barely hear music in the background. My eyes fell to the dark figure. I could tell he was male, but that was all. He wore a black hoodie that was pulled over his face. My body hadn't caught up to my mind just yet and lay immobile, despite my commands. Fear grew fiercely in my stomach as the guy slid his hand up my arm.

I tried to scream, but it came out as a mere mumble. His hands grazed across my breasts and sent my heart into overdrive. I needed to move. What was going on? I felt drugged. *Wait,* that was it. I must have been drugged. But the only drink I had came from… Dammit! Why'd I trust Cindy? I should have known she was a plant.

My thoughts slammed back into the moment when I felt his hand on the skin of my stomach. He lifted my shirt slightly as he began to fumble with the button on my pants. I had never in my life been so grateful to be wearing tight jeans. Panic gripped me as his finger played at my panty line. I knew this was going to end very badly if I couldn't regain control over my body soon.

I gathered all the energy I could. I knew I'd get one shot at calling for help before he'd cover my mouth, so it needed to be loud. I took one long, deep breath.

"Help!" I screamed with all I could muster. I didn't know if it'd be enough for someone to hear over the music. Just as I suspected, though, his hand flew to my mouth and no second chances were given. I tried moving my arms to fend off my attacker, but they were like hot rubber.

I was going to kill Cindy for this.

"You *are* sexy. I would have been up for this even if I weren't getting paid." His voice was breathy as his words settled over me. Paid? This whole thing was so screwed up. Had the cheerleaders *paid* to have me attacked?

I felt the pressure of my jeans release as he managed to unbutton them. Panic and fear choked me as my stomach rolled violently. He inched my pants down over my hips.

"Get the hell away from her!" I heard Jason yell. I could have cried in relief at that moment. The guy jerked back and raced out of sight. Jason leaned down over me. "Beth, are you all right?"

I couldn't speak. The relief had relaxed my muscles and sleep was impossible to fight.

CHAPTER SEVEN

SECRET VISIT

I awoke the next day not quite sure where I was. I was asleep in a bed much larger than my own. My head pounded as my eyes adjusted to the daylight that was streaming through a double paned glass door. Memories of the night before were fuzzy. The emotions of the night were recalled before the events finally hit me. The attack replayed in my head. Someone had paid to have me assaulted. *Gloria.* Anger planted a seed in my heart and grew beyond the capacity of my chest. No way was I going to just let this one go.

They had drugged me. They had all been in on it. I was going to get revenge on all the cheerleaders. But first, I had to figure out where I was. The last thing I remembered was Jason running my attacker off. Where had Jason taken me?

I stepped off the bed and through the bedroom door. It led to the living area of what I could now tell to be someone's pool house. Jason lay asleep on the couch. It did not appear to be comfortable for him due to his height and muscular build. He had one leg on the ground and one arm hanging from the edge. I felt appreciative to him for saving me last night, and I was touched that he had slept on the couch. I glanced over to the kitchen and decided I'd make him breakfast.

While searching through the cabinets, I found some pain killers and took a couple to get rid of my searing headache. Once I started frying bacon, I could hear Jason begin to stir. He followed the smell and found me in the kitchen.

"What are you doing?" He laughed.

"Making breakfast. As a thank you." I smiled sheepishly at him. I was suddenly embarrassed of my efforts. Breakfast was not nearly enough.

He came to stand behind me and slid his arms around my waist. "I love it."

My heart sped up at his proximity. Only when he moved away to get the orange juice out and set the table did it slow back to normal. I placed the bacon, eggs, and pancakes on the table. I made a smiley face out of my food before I layered it all in syrup and dug in. Jason laughed at my process as he ate his food like a normal person.

"So, do you remember what happened last night?" he asked.

I swallowed the bite I'd just taken a little too soon and it lumped up painfully as it went down. "Yes, I remember."

"We can call the cops if you want. It's totally up to you."

"Did you get a good look at the guy's face?" I asked hopefully.

"No, I didn't. I'm sorry," he admitted.

"Then, there's really no point. We don't know who it was. It'll only cause more trouble than it's worth. And as for the cheerleaders... I'm going to handle it," I told him.

"Okay." He smiled. "Would you like me to drive you home?"

"Yeah. Maybe if I get home before my aunt wakes up, she won't notice that I didn't come home last night." I held onto that wishful thinking until I tiptoed through the front door and saw Aunt Meredith on the couch.

"You need to call your mother," she asserted.

"Do I have to?" I groaned. "Can't we just keep this between the two of us?"

"Sorry, Beth. You're my responsibility now.

Besides, I called her when I woke up, so she already knows. She'll be angrier if you don't call and explain yourself." Aunt Meredith switched the television off. She gave me a small pat on my shoulder before disappearing upstairs to give me privacy. I inhaled deeply before dialing my mother's cell phone number.

"Beth?" she answered quickly.

"Yes, it's me. I'm really sorry-" I began, but was cut off by her rant.

"How dare you stay out all night and not call your aunt! Do you know how worried I was when she told me this morning? Anything could have happened to you and it would be nine hours before I could get to you. Where the hell were you last night, young lady?" It all came out in one breath, so it took me a moment to concept that she had asked a question. "Well?"

"Look, I just went to a party last night and it got to be late, so I crashed at a friend's house." I bent the truth as best I could.

"Were you drunk?" She sounded exasperated.

"No, Mom, I didn't even drink," I said, putting as much sincerity as I could into the words.

"That's it. Pack your things. I am coming to get you," she screeched through the phone, obviously not believing me.

"What are you talking about?"

"You are coming home! I'll just enroll you in private school," she stated.

"No, Mom, you and Dad can't afford that. I'm not going home. I'm sorry. I screwed up, but you can't just force me to move back home," I insisted. Even if my parents could afford the private school fees, there was no way the rumors wouldn't follow me.

"Oh, yes I can!" She was worked up, now. When she got this way, she just wanted to have control over everything. I knew it drove her crazy not being able to control my every move from so far away.

"Mom, I love you, but I am going to be eighteen in a few months."

"You are *still* seventeen and I am still your mother," she asserted.

"Mom, please." I pressed my fingers into my eyes in frustration. "I just started my senior year. I don't want to switch schools, *again*. I'm just getting into a routine here. I promise, no more parties."

She was silent for a moment as she contemplated my pleas. She let out a long sigh and I knew I had won. "Fine, but *one more mishap* and you're moving back home."

"Thank you," I muttered. Relief poured through me and I knew I needed to get off the phone before she changed her mind. "I have to get ready for work, so I'll call you back later. Love you."

"Love you, too," she said softly before hanging up.

My shower was a much needed one. A few leaves had burrowed themselves into the depths of my tangled hair. I dressed quickly in my uniform and hurried to work. The line was backed up when I strolled through the front entrance, so I rushed to clock in and help.

Hours flew by as the line finally dwindled down. Eventually, the coffee shop was left with only a few customers that lounged out on the couch with their macchiatos. As I scrubbed at a sticky mess near the whip cream, Courtney let out a small gasp.

"What?" I asked.

"Where did you get that necklace?" Her tone sounded accusatory, but I had no idea why.

"It was a gift." My hand instinctively flew to the pendant that my secret admirer had given me.

"From who?" Her eyes burned through my hand that covered the necklace.

"What does it matter?" My heart sped up at the mention of the sender.

"Because Emily had that exact necklace," she said pointedly.

"Well, obviously, it's not the same one," I asserted, but doubt tickled the back of my mind. She didn't respond, but her scowl didn't leave her face. I darted to the bathroom and stared at my gifts in the mirror. I wore all of them today. I examined the necklace closely. Could it be the same necklace? No, that was insane. That would mean whoever killed her was sending me the gifts. Gifts from dead girls. I shuddered.

The earrings suddenly seemed familiar to me. Had I seen them somewhere other than the mall? I searched my memory until I came across one that nearly made me scream. The girl on the news. She had been wearing these in her picture. My stomach rolled at the thought. No, I was remembering wrong. Courtney planted this idea in my head. All the same, I removed the jewelry and tossed them into the garbage.

Back in the dining area, I grabbed a broom and swept around all the empty tables.

"Hey, stranger," I heard a familiar voice say from behind me.

I whirled around and my suspicion was confirmed. *Amanda.* As in, my ex-best friend, Amanda. As in, the one who was *supposed* to drive that night. As in, the girl who ruined my life. *That Amanda.* How did she find me? And now that she had, what the hell did she want?

"What are you doing here, Amanda?" I snapped.

She flinched at my tone and glanced away.

"I just…" She paused to take a breath. "Can we talk in private?"

"I'm working," I asserted.

"It'll only take a few minutes. Don't you get a break or anything?" Her eyes pleaded with me. I wanted to tell her to screw off, but I felt a tiny tug at my heart.

"Fine, you got five minutes." I waved over to Susan to let her know I was taking my break. She nodded, so I led Amanda to the back entrance, not wanting anyone to overhear our conversation. I turned to her and gave her a stern expression. "How did you find me?"

"I know you don't have much extended family, but you stayed with your aunt that one summer, so I thought maybe. I looked her up, and then when I showed up, she told me you worked here," she explained.

"So, what do you want?" My jaw tightened

in irritation at the obvious attempt at delaying an explanation for her sudden appearance.

"I wanted to apologize." She gulped back what sounded like a lump in her throat. "After Tray died, I was a mess."

"How do you think I felt? He was *my* boy-friend!" I shot.

"I loved him, too! He was one of my best friends." She crossed her arms over her chest.

"*I* was your best friend." My throat tightened over the words. "I needed you to be there for me and I would have been there for you. But instead, you lashed out, like you always do. You hated me for his death, so you made sure everyone else did, too."

"I know. I'm sorry. I wish I could take it back." Guilt was etched into her face.

"Well, you can't. Life doesn't work that way. You screwed up and you have to deal with the consequences. I'm dealing with mine. Go home and deal with yours." I turned my back on her. I'd only taken a couple of steps when I heard her speak again.

"Do you remember why we became friends?" Her voice sounded small and childlike.

"It doesn't matter," I declared.

"It does. Do you remember?" she insisted.

"Everyone thought we were sisters because we looked so much alike." My words became softer until I was barely whispering.

"And neither of us had siblings, so we decided to be sisters," she said, finishing the story for me. My chest tightened at the fond memory. I twisted back around to fix a glare on her.

"If that's how sisters treat each other, then I'm glad I'm an only child," I asserted. I could tell my words hurt her. She whimpered quietly as I left her alone behind the coffee shop.

Unshed tears stung at my eyes for the rest of my shift. I didn't unleash them until I was in bed that night. Then, it was all I could do not to flood my bedroom. They came hard and heavy until my eyes were red and swollen. It was still early, but emotional exhaustion overtook me.

Jared sits at the edge of the creek with his feet in the water. I slide off my sandals and join him. I bite my lip as I watch the waves splash around my ankles. Jared slips his arm around my waist and tugs me closer to him.

"Are you okay?" he asks.

"No," I answer honestly. I'm not sure if I'll ever be okay again.

"Why didn't you call the cops after your attack?" Jared's voice is soft as his breath caresses my neck.

"Why bother? I don't know who it was. If I go to

the cops, then it'll spread around school," I tell him.

"What if he tries it again?" Jared's words drip with concern.

"Don't worry. I won't be attending any more parties." I give him a reassuring smile. This doesn't seem to ease his worry, but he remains silent. I shift so I can see his face. "Thank you for waking me." I tuck my hair behind my ear.

"Don't thank me for that." His tone is clipped.

"Why not?" I frown.

"I couldn't help you. I couldn't do anything." He sounds angry with himself and I don't understand why.

"But you did help me. It would have been... just awful if I hadn't woken up." I press my lips to his cheek. His frown flutters upward into a smile. His bright blue eyes study my face as emotions stir within them.

"What are you thinking about right now?" I ask with deep interest.

"You." His smoky tone causes my body to warm delectably. His eyes gaze at my mouth with an intensity that vibrates right through me.

"Jared?" I ask, drawing his eyes back to mine.

"Yes?" Our eyes mirror the yearning we each hold.

"Why do I dream of you?"

"Because I want you to." His answer causes me to inhale sharply. Could it be true? No, I'm only hearing the answer that I want to hear. I lay my head on his shoulder *and let out a sigh of contentment.*

"I wish that were true," I mumble to him.

My eyes flew open in a panic. The feeling I was being watched pulsated through every muscle. I leapt out of bed to switch on my bedroom light. Again, it was empty. I wasn't relieved, though. I truly felt someone had been in my room. My eyes searched for anything out of place until they landed on my window. It was wide open. I never opened the window, so there was no way I could have left it that way. I rushed over and stuck my head outside. I glanced around into the darkness of the moonless night but couldn't see anything. I was on the second floor, so it didn't make sense that anyone could enter my room through the window. Then again, the tree in the yard was so close that if someone did climb it, they could easily jump onto the roof that extended below my window. The thought made me shudder.

A tiny shimmer of light caught my attention. My eyes flitted to a small object on the top of the roof. It was close enough that I reached out my arm and picked it up easily. It was a candy package. My bedroom light reflected off the plastic. The writing on the package said, *Mega Bruiser Jawbreaker.* How did this get up here? I didn't even know they sold these anymore. Did the wind blow it up here, or was it left by someone?

I yanked the window down with shaky hands. I locked it, triple checking the action. However, it wasn't enough reassurance for me to fully relax. My eyes remained fixated on the window. Was I going crazy? What proof did I have that someone had been watching me sleep? Had someone actually been in my room, so close to me, while I lay there helpless? My gut feelings weren't exactly reliable. And what about the jewelry? No, I refused to think about that. It was far too disturbing to even allow those thoughts to enter my mind.

I tried to steer my mind away from the fear that I couldn't seem to shake, so I let my thoughts drift to my recent encounter with Amanda. Had I been a complete bitch to her? *Yeah,* I answered myself. Did she honestly deserve it? *Probably.* I, no doubt, could have been a little more sympathetic to her, though. She was right that she had been close with Tray. They were friends before Tray and I even started dating. Sure, she had completely stabbed me in the back, but she tried to apologize.

Her words aren't enough, I thought bitterly. It

wasn't just her words, though. She had driven nine hours on the *off-chance* that I was here. Regret permeated me.

It was only just barely dawn, but I needed to call Amanda. I tiptoed down the steps trying to be as quiet as possible. I dialed her cell phone number and listened as it rang. I wasn't surprised when it went to voicemail.

A recording of her peppy voice sang through the phone. "Hi, you've reached Amanda. I'm either at school or at cheer practice. Either way, I'll call you back." I smiled as I remembered the day she had recorded that greeting. We had just made the cheer squad and were super excited to let everyone know.

"Hey, Amanda. It's Beth. I'm sorry for the way I acted yesterday. I know it's early, but if you could call me back at this number when you wake up, I'd really appreciate it." I hung up the phone as a sad feeling spread through me. I hoped she would call me back. She probably hated me again after what I said.

I wasn't sure what to do with myself for the day. It was Sunday, so I didn't have school, and I was scheduled off, so no work either. I decided that I should probably make up to Aunt Meredith for not coming home Friday night. I deep cleaned the house for the next few hours until my back ached and my muscles cried for a break. I picked up the phone and dialed Amanda's cell phone again. No answer. I dialed her home phone.

"Hello?" Amanda's mother answered after a few rings.

"Hi, is Amanda there?"

"She's out of town this weekend. She won't be back until late tonight. You could try calling her cell phone," her mother suggested.

"Okay, thank you." I hung up before her mother could ask me to identify myself.

Where did Amanda go after she left the coffee shop yesterday? Why would she not go straight home? Maybe this was only a short stop on her original trip. I sighed. The ball was in her court now. She could either call me back so we could talk it out or she could just ignore me. There was nothing more I could do about it.

My mind was torn from my thoughts when I heard Aunt Meredith's footsteps descending the stairs. By the way she was dressed, I could tell she was on her way to morning service. She acknowledged my progress with a grateful smile before she headed out the door. The rest of the day was spent cleaning Aunt Meredith's attic. I tackled the project with full force to keep my mind clear of everything.

I returned the china doll to where I had placed it in the attic. This was its new home. Stacking boxes, I came across one that had the words "photo albums" written in black marker on it. Curiosity got the better of me as I tugged it open. I glanced through a few albums, but there was one that had a ton of pictures of me in it and I decided to keep it out for a more detailed look through.

Once I was finished cleaning, I spread out on the couch with the photo album in hand. I opened it to the first page. There were a couple of pictures of me and Mom. I was seven and wearing the pink, fluffy dress that had later been destroyed during a gruesome mud fight with Jared. Mom wore a smile, but I could see the worry in her eyes. That summer had been hard on her. My mind flashed back to a conversation I had overheard between my mom and my aunt. Aunt Meredith wanted to talk about funeral arrangements in case the surgery didn't go well and my mom was having none of it. I was too young back then to understand and my mom had put on a brave front for me. This picture was proof of it. A pang of guilt hit me as I recalled how much trouble I had been.

I turned the page and inhaled sharply. There were pictures of Jared and me. Clearly, I had taken these pictures without adult supervision because half of them were fuzzy. There was one where, in my attempt to take a selfie of Jared and me, half my face was cut off. Huge smiles plastered our faces and we appeared to be having a blast. I grinned down at our little faces. There were tons of pictures that I had taken. Some of the tree by the creek. Some of random frogs we had caught.

There was one picture that caught my eye, though. It was fuzzy, so I couldn't be sure, but I thought I saw a figure standing in the background of it. Jared and I were too busy laughing to notice it, but it appeared someone had been watching us. The thought sent icy shivers throughout my body.

I flipped the page hoping I had gotten a clearer shot of the figure. It was in a couple of others, but they were just as fuzzy, if not more. I told myself it was probably just Jared's dad or something, but the unease that had settled in my stomach refused to move along. I came across a blank space where a picture had clearly been. *That's peculiar.* Luck was on my side, for once, as Aunt Meredith waltzed in right at that moment.

"Hello, Beth. What are you looking at?" she questioned.

"A photo album I found in the attic," I told her. "Hey, do you know what happened to this picture." I pointed to the empty spot.

"Oh, gosh, I don't know. Those have been up there for a while. You know what, though? Steve put them all on a disc for me a few years back. He said it was just in case anything ever happened to the pictures themselves, but I don't know anything about computers. You can check it, if you like. The disc is on the shelf with all my tapes," she explained. Steve was my older cousin who was the tech guy of the family. I nearly laughed at the notion that Aunt Meredith had placed the disc with her VHS tapes.

There wasn't a computer here, but I figured I could take it to school and use one of the library computers. It took a few moments to find the disc because Aunt Meredith owned more VHS tapes than I'd ever even seen in my life. I stuck the disc into my backpack so that I wouldn't forget to bring it the next day.

That night, I fell asleep instantly – after I double checked the locks on every window and every door. My dreams were filled with – surprise surprise – Jared. Not that I minded. Although, I was beginning to worry that I was having an entirely one-sided relationship that he had no clue about. My concerns weren't enough for me to try to stop having the dreams because, honestly, I was enjoying my dream relationship. I loved the dream cuddling. I loved the dream kissing. I loved Ja – nope. Do not finish that sentence. That was heartbreak territory. *You do not love him*, I scolded myself. It's not real. *You cannot love a fantasy*. My heart tightened in disagreement.

CHAPTER EIGHT

SECRET REVENGE

I woke the next morning in a determined mood. I knew exactly what I would do to the cheerleaders. Revenge was going to be sweet. I gathered up the supplies I needed and stuffed it all into my backpack. There was only one thing missing, but I knew Jonathan could get it for me. I gave him a quick call to confirm that he would bring it. Everything was ready.

I spent the first part of the day ignoring Gloria's sneers. Her cronies – aka all the cheerleaders – and Gloria herself couldn't seem to stop with the nasty under-the-breath comments. I knew I'd get them back right after third period, the one that was designated for their cheerleading practice. I waited until they were all in the showers before I slipped into the locker room. Earlier in the day, I had Jonathan help me fill the fire sprinklers with purple dye. Now, it was time to put my plan into action. I gathered all the clothing I could find and stuffed it all into a garbage sack. I tiptoed over to the showers and grabbed the towels from the hooks. I tossed the sack over to Jonathan who stood outside the door. He hurried off to hide it.

The next part would be the hardest for me to do silently. I unzipped the duffel bag that Jonathan had given me and held in my squeal as a six-foot snake slithered out right toward the showers. I shuddered, extremely glad I wasn't on the receiving end of this prank. I was ready to jet out of there, but I had one last thing to do. I pulled the lever on the fire alarm causing the alarms to sound and the sprinklers began to spew out purple water. I raced out the door before I got wet and was caught purple-handed.

I joined the gathered students outside and waited for the grand finale. It didn't take long. High-pitched screams could be heard a mile away. Purple, naked bodies hauled ass out of the locker room and out onto the grass in front of shocked onlookers. It took everyone a moment to react, but when they did, phones were being pulled out as the crowd jeered.

The girls squealed in horror as they attempt-ed to cover as much of themselves as they could with just their hands. They stood in a confused mess not knowing what to do. If they went back into the locker room, they would have to face the snake. Gloria's purple/red face found mine. I smiled to show her I had won. She glared at me with a hatred very few could match. Finally, they raced into the boys' locker room.

The students broke out into loud, hysterical laughter and commentary. This would be all over social media, not that I would be able to see any of it. I might have felt bad if they hadn't drugged me and tried to have me *raped*. No, this was totally justified.

My heart leapt in my chest when I spotted Jared. I darted over to him. "Hey, did you see what happened?" I questioned, unable to keep the smug grin from my face.

"You mean that epic prank? Yeah, I think half the school did." His tone seemed impressed, as his lips pulled into a boyish grin.

"Thanks." I bit my lip. "So, I found some pictures of us when we were kids. I guess my mom let me use her camera."

"Yeah, I remember that. You probably took a million pictures that summer." He laughed.

"It does appear I went pretty overboard. Well, I just thought you might want to see them." I reached out to touch his arm, but he jerked away before I could. Hurt and embarrassment seared my chest. "Right, well, I better get to class." I rushed off before he could say anything to make it worse.

That heartbreak I was talking about earlier? Yeah, this was it. Tears stung my eyes, but I refused to let them fall. *I had fallen in love with a fantasy*, I finally admitted. *It was all in my head.* The thoughts hurt, but I knew it was for my own good. I needed to step back into reality. I took a deep breath and headed for my fourth period class.

The cheerleaders were nowhere to be found after the prank that day. Apparently, purple was not their color. Considering it was the color for our school's biggest rival and that the game against them was this Friday, I couldn't blame them for not wanting to show off their new *Barney the Dinosaur* look. I secretly hoped they'd be stained for weeks. I doubted I'd get that lucky, but as long as it lasted through Friday, I felt satisfied. Unfortunately, I'd have to deal with their retaliation, but I found that it didn't concern me. They had gotten through my defenses once, but it wouldn't happen again. I was ready for anything they threw my way.

I thoroughly thanked Jonathan later at

mathletes practice. He had managed to retrieve his pet snake once everyone cleared out. I was relieved that the snake wouldn't be aimlessly wandering the hallways.

"Alright, back to the business at hand. In case any of you have been sleeping for the past couple of weeks, we have a competition on Wednesday. It starts early and ends late, so we'll be leaving tomorrow and not returning until Thursday. Please, be sure you all have your release forms signed by your parents by then. If not, you can't go and we need each and every one of us if we are going to win," Jonathan announced. I tugged out my release form. I had gotten Aunt Meredith to sign it last week. I handed it to Jonathan who collected all the forms.

I was excited and nervous about the meet. If we won, we'd get to move onto the state competition. They hadn't won any competitions since "Vegas" had left, so it would be a huge deal if we did. Jonathan seemed confident that I was their golden ticket. It was surprising to me because I never realized I was talented at math. I mean, I knew I made A's in class, but that didn't really mean anything. Maybe I had just been too focused on cheerleading to pay it too much attention.

I made my way to the library once mathletes practice was over. I chose a computer in the corner so I'd have some privacy. I popped the disc in and searched through all the pictures. There were tons since Steve had scanned *all* of Aunt Meredith's pictures. Finally, I got to the portion that had me and Jared. I clicked through them, one by one, until I came across a picture that wasn't in the album.

This was the missing picture.

It was one of me by myself. Jared must have been holding the camera. My hair was wet and I was wearing a bright yellow bathing suit. My eyes instantly went to my right shoulder. There was a scabbed over wound. It appeared to be maybe a week old.

This was right after I got hurt.

Why was this picture missing? Perhaps, it just got misplaced, but that explanation wasn't settling well with me. I couldn't put my finger on it, but I felt like there was something else going on here.

Later that night, Jared was once again in my dream.

"I can't do this anymore," I announce. His mood turns poignant.

"Please, stay," he pleads. I shake my head, feeling

torn.

"No," I whisper as I force the dream away. The creek vanishes, then the tree disappears, and finally, Jared fades away into a shimmering light. My stomach clenches at the loss, but I remind myself it is not real. But it feels real. I fold in on myself as tears pour down my face. This is how it has to be.

My heartbreak followed me into my wakeful state. I clutched my doll as I let a few leftover tears fall. *Hold on! Doll?* Terror burst through my veins as I leapt from my bed so fast that I nearly tripped over my blanket. There she was. The china doll sat in the middle of my pillow. The overwhelming urge to burn the evil thing pulsated through me. I may not have been able to destroy the doll, but I could bury it. I wrapped the doll in an airtight plastic bag making sure to keep it facing away from me the entire time. I dug a hole in the back yard and threw it inside, covering it back up with dirt.

If the stupid thing resurrected one more time, I didn't care if it was my grandmother's, I was going to burn it. Not just burn it. I was going to douse it in kerosene then watch it burn until I knew it was nothing more than ash.

I didn't see Jared before I joined the math-letes in the van that was to take us to our hotel. I knew it was for the best. I needed to distance myself from him if I was going to get over this stupid crush. It was a good thing the competition was being held a couple of hours away. I could use a few days to clear my head.

I sighed as I stared out the window into the evening. As the sun set, various shades of pink sparkled across the sky and the first leaves of fall blew through the air. Yawns filled the van as we drove up to our hotel. It was a decent size with maybe five floors. Mr. Stephenson checked in our rooms while we gathered our luggage. He handed us our keys. I was the only one who got my own room since I was the only girl. I guess that was one benefit.

I was more than ready for sleep by the time I changed into my tank top and shorts and crawled into bed. My brain hurt from all the practice problems Jonathan forced upon us these last couple of days. I felt exhausted and it would be an early morning for us. I closed my eyes and was relieved not to see Jared. Instead, my head was filled with mathematical equations and stressful competition situations.

I awoke with a start in the middle of the night. Drowsiness didn't allow my mind to hold onto a single thought. My bladder screamed at me so I rolled out of bed for the bathroom. As I strolled over to the bathroom, I noticed the door to my room was slightly ajar. Not quite open but not quite shut. My heart slammed into overdrive. I know I pushed the door all the way shut when I came in. I darted to the door and shoved it closed. How could this be happening *here?* Maybe this was all in my head and I was a lot more careless than I believed myself to be. My clenched gut told me it wasn't buying it.

I rushed into the bathroom like something or someone was after me. After peeing, I stood over the sink as I washed my hands feeling calmer and slightly silly for running in here like a cliché horror film chick. Drying my hands on a towel, I realized my strap was down on my top and my scar was in full view. I used my thumb to move my strap back into place and, as I did, it brushed across my skin. *My scar was wet.* What the hell? I grabbed a rag and dried off the spot. That was strange. Had I drooled in my sleep? That was such an odd place for it to land, though. I couldn't shake the eerie feeling that there was more to it than that.

I forced myself back to sleep after checking just once to be sure the door was still closed. I needed every ounce of brainpower for the competition.

The next day was filled with stressful excitement. Our team proved to be well above most of the competition. We won second place, which was enough for us to move ahead. That night, we celebrated in Jonathan's room. We gorged on double cheese stuffed crust pizza and sugar filled soda while watching a movie about a card counting genius who made millions of dollars in Vegas. Everyone seemed to be thinking of their former teammate.

"So, no one has heard from Vegas? Like, at all?" I asked out of curiosity.

"No," Jonathan answered in a sad voice.

"How do you know he ran away, then? I mean, if you guys were such good friends, why wouldn't he contact you?" I pointed out. Jonathan bit the inside of his cheek and I knew I had hit a sore spot. I regretted mentioning it.

"Wishful thinking." He glued his eyes back to the television, but I could tell his mind was somewhere else. I don't know why it took me this long to realize that they were *choosing* to believe he had run away. It was easier to believe that he had hit it big and lived on some tropical island somewhere than to believe the worst. I nodded and remained silent for the rest of the movie.

"Alright, guys. Time to head back to your rooms. Especially you, Beth," Mr. Stephenson said as he popped his head into the room.

Once I was back in my room, I fully shut the door and dragged a chair over to prop it underneath the door handle. *Just in case*. It gave me enough peace of mind to fall asleep. A few hours later, I jumped awake when the chair fell to the floor. *Someone is trying to get in*, I thought to myself. I grabbed my high heeled shoe for a weapon and tiptoed in the darkness. The door was left ajar and the chair was toppled to the ground, but no one was around. I scanned the empty hallway outside my door. Nothing. I guess the chair scared away whoever had tried to get in. The question was, how did they get a room key?

I decided I wanted to know. I threw on some jeans and rushed over towards the elevator. Fear trickled down my skin as I realized the intruder might still be here. My eyes darted around me, but there wasn't a living soul to be seen. I pressed the button for the elevator twenty more times – there was no way I was taking the stairs – before it finally opened its doors for me. I hopped into it and pressed the first-floor button, but nothing seemed to happen. I assaulted the close doors button with my thumb, terrified someone would jump in.

I nearly screamed when a hand darted through the closing doors at the last second. The doors slowly reopened and a man in his early thirties stepped in. He had furry eyebrows with a nose too large for his face. I looked away from him and stared intently at the lit button. My pulse raced with anxiety as the humming of the elevator filled my ears. The elevator dang as we reached the first floor and the stranger scurried off without a single glance my way.

I strolled up to the front desk where a young girl who appeared to have just gotten out of high school was on her cellphone. She told whoever she was speaking with to hold on a moment before turning her attention to me.

"How can I help you?" she asked in a polite voice.

"I was wondering, did you give a key to anyone for room 415?" I questioned.

"I haven't seen anyone tonight," she responded.

I thought about it and remembered last night. "What about last night? After we checked in, did anyone ask for a room key for 415?"

"Oh, yeah. Someone did last night. He said he was with your school and needed another room key. He showed me his school ID," she said defensively.

"Do you remember his name?" My chest tightened. *Someone had been in my room.* I wasn't crazy. And if someone had been in there this time, did that mean I was right the other times?

"No, sorry." She shrugged.

"Well, what did he look like?"

"I don't know? Cute." She was unhelpful as ever.

"What about your cameras? Can you look at them?" I was desperate to know who had gotten into my room.

"Sorry, only corporate has access to those. You'll have to file an official request and that could take months." Her words deflated me.

"Well, thanks." *For nothing,* I silently added.

Once I was back in my room, I propped the chair back up and spent the rest of the night watching old movies. There was no way I could sleep knowing someone had a key to my room. I'd nap on the van ride back to school. Since we wouldn't be getting back until lunch time, the mathletes were excused from school Thursday. Plus, we had a three-day weekend so I wouldn't have to be back in school until Monday.

I pondered who could have gotten the room

key. He had a school ID. The only ones here with school ID's were the mathletes. Of course, she had described him as "cute" so unless awkward nerd was her type, I doubted she was referring to one of them. What other option was there? I groaned as frustration and fear threatened to pull me into a panic. I took long, deep breaths as my eyes stayed glued to the door. My tense muscles expected someone to barge in at any moment.

Someone could have made a fake school ID, I thought. But who would go through all the trouble just to get to me? It didn't make any sense. If it was someone who knew me, then they knew where I lived. *They knew where I lived.* The thought carved into my mind in a painful sawing fashion. *Was it the same person who was in my room those two nights?* The notion terrified me, causing my stomach to roll. *No, I'm just being paranoid, like always,* I assured myself. But was I? The chair was proof that someone *had* tried to get in my room. Plus, someone *had* gotten a key last night.

I wanted so badly to stock it all up to stress, but I just couldn't. One girl was dead and one girl was missing *Girls that looked like me.* Had they all just caught the attention of the wrong person? *Had I?* I gulped back a lump that formed in my throat. If that was the case, what should I do? Go to the police? It's not like I exactly have a solid case. I had stupidly tossed the only evidence I might have had in the trash. No, they'd be no help to me. I'd just have to be more observant and stay prepared. I refused to be the victim to whatever sick game was being played or worse, the victim of some depraved pervert.

CHAPTER NINE

TWO CAN KEEP A SECRET...

The next morning, I packed my bag in anticipation of our departure. How did I manage to leave my clothes all over the room? Outfit choices were not a friend to me. I sighed as I grabbed a shirt that had managed to get knocked under the bed. I heard a crinkling noise as I brought it to my tote bag. I shook the shirt out and something fell from it. I took a sharp intake of breath when I saw what it was.

A Mega Bruiser Jawbreaker wrapper.

My mind flashed back to the last one I found. It had been right outside my bedroom. This couldn't be a coincidence. My hands shook as I stuffed the empty wrapper into my pocket.

As soon as our van arrived back in Middleton the next day, I walked to the store. I had a general idea of what I wanted to buy but wasn't sure how much I could get being under eighteen. I knew pepper spray was a must. They even had it in bright pink. In the end, the only weapons my age allowed me to buy were the pepper spray, a large kitchen knife, and a baseball bat. It wasn't exactly a handgun, but it was better than high heels.

Once home, I placed the kitchen knife under my pillow, propped the baseball bat next to my bed, and set the pepper spray on my side table. I found some scrap wood out in the shed and used some to wedge between the top of the bottom half of the window and its upper frame. This felt more secure than the small latch. I installed the new door handle I bought. Now, I had a lock. I glanced around at all my efforts. I wasn't sure if it would be enough to allow for any actual sleep, but it was all I could do.

It was evening before Aunt Meredith came waltzing in with a few shopping bags. One bag held some freshly checked out library books while the other had a few cat toys. She instantly called her cats and began playing with them.

"Hi, Beth. How was the competition?" she queried once she spotted me on the stairs.

"Good. We placed second," I informed her. "Did anyone call for me?" I worried the inside of my cheek. I had hoped Amanda would call me back.

"Oh, actually, Jason called for you on Tuesday. I said I'd have you call him back." She rubbed the underbelly of a very content tabby.

"Thanks," I told her and headed for the phone.

Instead of calling Jason, though, I dialed Amanda's cell phone again. This time, it went straight to voicemail. *That was strange.* She *never* had her phone turned off. I supposed it could have died, but even that seemed unlikely for Amanda. I left her a short message and hung up. I thought about calling Jason back but decided that it could wait until tomorrow. I was exhausted and ready to get some sleep.

Unfortunately, sleep that night was less than restful. I would sleep about ten minutes before jerking awake at any small noise. All in all, the night was uneventful if not full of suspense. It left me more tired than rested.

After a quick breakfast, I showered which seemed to help relax my nerves. I wrapped myself in a towel and jogged down the stairs. I needed to call Jason before I forgot. I glanced at the notepad that Aunt Meredith had jotted his number down on and dialed.

"Hello?" he answered in a raspy voice. I could tell I had woken him.

"Hey, it's Beth. Did I wake you?"

"No, well, yeah, but it's okay." I could hear his smile through the phone.

"Oh, didn't know you'd still be lazing in bed. I just assumed you'd be getting back from your morning run," I said teasingly.

"So, you were hoping to catch me fresh from the shower then?" His tone held a sensual aspect that caused me to picture him in only a towel. A heat spread through my body at the mental visual. His voice cut the long silence my thoughts had created. "You want me to send you a pic to help with that fantasy you're conjuring up of me right now?"

I blushed as my mind scrambled for a response. I cleared my throat, deciding to change the subject. "My aunt said you called for me while I was out of town," I stated.

"I did," he said with a knowing laugh. I waited for a moment for him to elaborate, but he didn't.

"So, what's up?" I queried.

"Well, it's kind of last minute now, but I was hoping to take you to dinner tonight after the game."

"Oh." I gripped the phone tighter in my hand, so as not to drop it.

"Is that a good 'oh' or a bad 'oh'?" His voice sounded vulnerable and my heart clenched. It was just dinner, right? Then, why was I hesitating? Because of Jared? Jared was clearly not interested and here was a guy, a sexy one at that, who had shown his interest on more than one occasion. A guy who had *saved* me. Didn't *he* deserve to be given a chance?

"A good 'oh.' What time are you picking me up?" I questioned.

"It's an early game. How's eight-thirty sound?" His overly excited tone made me grin in response.

"Sounds great," I responded.

That evening, my room appeared to have been victim to a tornado. My clothes were strewn everywhere in attempt to find the perfect outfit. The only thing remotely cute enough for a dinner date was a strapless dress that was tight at my waist but flowed out at my hips. The strapless part was a mucho problemo. I *never* wore anything strapless. If an outfit didn't cover my scar, I wouldn't wear it. This dress must have been something my mother bought me.

I tugged the dress on. It complimented my figure perfectly. If I kept my hair down and over my shoulder the whole night, it might just work. I straightened my hair and pulled back only pieces, holding them in place with some bobby pins. Finally satisfied, I stepped out of my small bathroom. I let out a squeal of surprise to see Jared.

"What are you doing here?" My heart still pounded in my chest from the fright. I glanced at my bedroom door. I had left it unlocked.

What is the point of having a lock if you don't use it? I scolded myself.

"Please, tell me I heard wrong. Tell me you aren't going on a date with Jason." His eyes were wide and held an intense mix of emotions.

"I can't do that." I moved past him, gathering my things. It was eight and Jason would be arriving soon.

"Why are you doing this?" His voice held a desperate tone I hadn't heard in it before.

"Why do you care? You obviously don't want anything to do with me. You can't even stand to touch me," I shot. That last part poured salt on a tiny wound in my chest.

"That's not true," he whispered. "I want you more than anything."

I stopped everything I was doing and twisted around. His face held a sadness I couldn't understand. "If that's true, then why do you treat me like I'm diseased?"

"Don't go on the date. Stay and I'll tell you everything," he pleaded with me.

"You've got five minutes to convince me to stay," I told him.

"Jason is deranged. He's a murderer." Jared's voice was low as it reached my ears.

"What? I don't understand." That was the last thing I had expected Jared to say. "How do you know?"

"Because he killed me to cover up his secret." Jared watched me carefully.

"He killed you?" My eyebrow quirked up in disbelief. "You're insane."

"It's true. I am, I mean was, his brother. He kills girls at our father's cabin. I caught him doing sick things to that poor girl. I tried to stop him and he killed me. You can't go with him," Jared asserted passionately.

"You expect me to believe all that? That you're a ghost?" I shook my head with overwhelming emotions.

"I can prove it." He stepped closer to me. "Let me see your hand."

I hesitated briefly, but then slowly lifted my hand. I watched as his hand closed the distance between us until his skin finally pressed against mine.

"I don't get it." My eyes returned to Jared's. His face was covered in astonishment.

"I-" He continued staring down at our touching hands. "I've never been able to touch anyone before. I've always gone right through them." He lifted his other hand to cup my face. He held his breath as his finger traced across my cheek.

"You realize how insane you sound, right?" I didn't know what to believe. Obviously, he wasn't a ghost. Not that there was even a moment that I had believed that, but still.

"I know, but you have to believe me. Jason is psychotic. He's going to kill you," he declared.

My gut clenched as my heart sped up. Was he telling the truth? No, because then that would mean he was dead and *that* I refused to believe.

"I'm sorry." I shook my head.

"You promised you wouldn't run," he whispered.

Those words sounded familiar and my mind raced to connect them with a memory. My eyes widened. He was right. I *had* promised him that. Except, it had happened in one of my dreams.

"How did you know that?" I demanded.

"Because I was really there," he admitted.

"I'm sorry. I know it was wrong. I just… I wanted to hold you, to be able to touch you." My mind raced with this new information he provided me with. *It was actually him.* So, then the feelings I had developed were real. But, then he really *was* a ghost.

My only two options at the moment were to either believe Jared or to conclude that he was absolutely out of his mind. But then how did he know about a conversation I'd had with dream Jared? I had never told him about it. And what about Jason? Could he really be a murderer? But, if he was intent on killing me, then why did he go through the trouble of saving me? It didn't make any sense.

"But we're touching now." I referred to his hand that still cupped my cheek.

"I didn't know. I wish I had." Longing filled his eyes. He leaned in and placed a soft kiss on my lips.

"This is all too much." I took a step back. "And before you say anything, I'm *not* running. I just need some time. You dropped a bomb on me, just now."

"Are you going on the date?" Jared pressed.

"Yes," I told him. He began to argue, but I cut him off. "We're just going to dinner, not to some cabin."

"Please, don't go." His voice held an audible panic.

"I'm sorry. I need to hear his side of things." I frowned.

"You *cannot* confront him, Lizzie." His alarm escalated off the charts.

"I'm not," I assured. "I'm just going to ask him some casual questions."

"I'm *begging* you not to go." He placed his hand on my shoulder.

"When he killed the other girls, did he kidnap them?" I questioned.

"No, he invited them on a romantic weekend," Jared answered with a puzzled expression.

"Well, he's only invited me to dinner. No mention of a romantic weekend," I placated. "Why don't you just wait for me here? We can talk more when I get back."

He let out a frustrated sigh. "Fine, but take that." He gestured toward my pepper spray. I nodded and stuck it in my purse.

We heard a knock at the door, and Jared's eyes gripped mine. His expression implored me not to go, but his voice remained silent. I moved toward the door. With what seemed like a sudden impulse, Jared darted across the room. He wrapped his arms around me and placed his lips to mine. Passion filled his every movement as his mouth moved with mine. He pressed harder into me and I became wedged between his body and the wall. My heart pounded as little sparks ignited from his lips and sizzled over mine. Need overwhelmed us both as I responded to his kisses. Another knock broke us from the moment.

"I want to hold you here and not let you go." His voice was heavy, as if all his emotion weighed a ton.

"Please don't," I said, even though part of me wanted that, too. My emotions were confused with what was real. Being near him was obviously jumbling my thoughts. I needed space from Jared to figure this all out.

He sighed in resignation as he stepped back. "Be careful."

I nodded before hurrying out of the room. I slid out the front door where Jason stood waiting for me. A wide smile spread across his face, showing off his dimples.

"You look perfect," he complimented, his eyes grazing over my bare shoulders.

"Thanks," I said awkwardly.

I gathered my hair back over my right

shoulder to cover my scar. I was suddenly second guessing my decision to continue this date. I could always pretend I had food poisoning or something. No, it was too late. Besides, if Jared *was* insane, then Jason didn't deserve to be blown off like that.

Dusk devoured the sun as Jason drove us to a restaurant in Nampa. I stared out the window in an attempt to gather my thoughts. Darkness swam outside the car. Summer bugs fluttered through the wind created by our seventy-mile-per-hour speed. After about ten minutes, I finally worked up the nerve to speak.

"So, tell me more about yourself. What sort of movies do you like? What's your favorite color? Do you have any siblings?" I tried to sound casual, but I could feel my voice tighten on the word "siblings."

"Okay. Well, I prefer horror flicks, my favorite color is red, and I have one brother," he listed. My stomach clenched at his last answer. *He has a brother.*

"I didn't know you have a brother," I said, prompting him for more information.

"Yeah, he has... issues. He ran away last year and we haven't heard from him since," he said smoothly. I studied his expression, but he seemed genuine. Either he was an amazing liar or he was being honest.

"Why did he run away?" I queried.

"Gambling addiction. He never could stay away from Vegas," Jason explained.

"Wait, is that your brother's nickname? Vegas?" Could Jared really be the Vegas everyone kept talking about?

"Yeah, he got that nickname after his gambling got him into trouble. He was a smart kid but never knew when to back off."

Jason's words made my stomach drop. Did he just refer to his brother in the *past tense?* Slip of the tongue, I'm sure. I attempted to slow my speeding heart, but it was untamable. I tried to keep my cool, but I never did have a good poker face. I glanced away from Jason so he wouldn't be able to see my expression. My eyes caught on something in the floorboard. I reached down to grab it, hoping it would distract me. Unfortunately, what I picked up only made my panic worse. *A Mega Bruiser Jawbreaker wrapper.* I gulped.

I casually stuck my hand into my purse to retrieve my pepper spray. Jason's eyes moved from the road to my face. My heart slammed against my ribcage and all I could hear was the sound of my own pulse beating in my ears. His eyes darted to my hand.

"Dammit, Beth. You couldn't just leave it alone," he roared. I gripped the pepper spray in my hand, but he didn't give me the opportunity to use it. Jason grabbed my hair and yanked my head backward. With a swift, hard thrust, he slammed my head against the dashboard. The world went dark.

CHAPTER TEN

SECRET MEMORIES

My head throbbed and my vision was fuzzy as I came to. I wasn't sure where I was exactly. It was pitch black aside from the moonlight that beamed in through a window about six feet above where I lay, which had to be on the floor. My hands were bound above my head and my dress was gone. That was all I could tell. I was tempted to scream for help but didn't want to alert Jason to my conscious state if he was nearby. I needed to get my hands out of the rope. My wrists were slender, so I usually was able to slide out of any sort of binding, but this was impressively tied. It felt like climbing rope or maybe rope that hunters used. Either way, it was tight and not going to come undone by simply wiggling it around. That was only going to rub my skin raw.

Loud footsteps echoed from outside the room I was in, causing my heart to soar into overdrive. Someone flicked on the light and my eyes burned as they dilated. Jason stood over me. He studied me carefully as I glanced at my surroundings. I was indeed lying on the floor. My wrists were bound to the leg of a bedpost. The room was small and the furnishings told me this was the cabin Jared had referred to.

Crap. I should have stayed. *I'm such an idiot.*

My attention shot back to Jason who crouched down next to me. "As much as I love to watch you sleep, I'm glad you're awake." He rolled a short table over to us. I screamed when I saw what lay atop of it. Knives of different sizes and shapes. He grinned at my outburst, but did nothing to stop me. "You can scream all you want. There's nothing but woods for miles around. No one will hear you." Panic choked me. The only person who knew I was here was Jared, and he was apparently dead. My stomach twisted in knots as terror permeated my body.

"What are you going to do to me?" My voice shook as my fear got the better of me.

"That is a good question. What am I going to do with you?" Jason seemed to be asking himself this. "Well, if you hadn't ruined my plans by being a nosy, little…" He inhaled as if to regain control over his temper. "Then I'd be more prepared. But life is full of surprises and now, here we are. So, to answer your question, we're just going with the flow."

I gulped to keep the rising bile down. He hadn't answered my question, but I got the gist that it wouldn't be pleasant for me. I glanced down at my body. I was in only my strapless bra and panties. I could see my dress in the corner of the room where he'd tossed it aside.

I noticed my legs were free so I began kicking at Jason. This seemed to excite him as he placed my legs between his while shifting on top of me.

"My favorite part is the fight." Deep pleasure grew within his eyes. I felt helpless as his hands brushed along my sides until they stopped at my shoulders. His movement became drudgingly slow as his finger traced along my scar.

"I've been searching for you for a long time, now," he mumbled as he concentrated on my scar.

"What are you talking about?" That familiar feeling that I had forgotten something important returned.

"You honestly don't remember, do you?" The corner of his mouth quirked up as I shook my head. "Well, let me help you out."

He grabbed a knife and I screeched, "No!" It was long and pointed. "Please, stop." He pressed its sharp edge into my shoulder directly on my scar. I wailed out in pain as he dragged it over my skin, reopening the old wound. Blood trickled down my shoulder and onto the floor. The memory was creeping up, but I still couldn't quite get to it. A dark smile shadowed his face as he lowered his head. I felt the urgent need to vomit as he pressed his tongue to the cut. He licked straight along the wound. His action triggered the memory and it plowed into my mind in a frenzied fashion. Memories overtook me as I was forced to relive the moment.

I am seven. I am playing at the creek like normal, waiting for Jared. I am brushing the dark hair of my favorite china doll. I think I hear him, so I twist around. The boy that stands there looks a little like Jared, but when he smiles, he has dimples. They instantly make me trust him. He asks me if I want to play a game. I nod. I love games. He tells me to lie down and close my eyes. I wonder if this is hide and seek. I do not ask but do as he tells me. I open my eyes, startled when he sits on my legs.

"What are you doing?" I ask him curiously.

"Playing the game. Close your eyes," he tells me. I feel no reason to be afraid, so I close them, once again. He tickles my shoulder and I giggle.

"Ouch!" I yell when I feel a sharp pain in my shoulder. My eyes open and I see blood. "Stop it! I don't want to play anymore," I cry out.

"You have to finish the game." His face seems scary, all of a sudden. He holds back my flailing arms as he leans down, placing his lips to my shoulder. I think he is kissing it to make it better, but something in his eyes tells me it's for something else. He licks it.

"Gross! Get off me!" I wiggle underneath him, but he is bigger than me. "Help!" I scream. His hands wrap around my throat and squeeze. I can't breathe. My head is getting dizzy.

"Jason, stop!" I hear Jared's small voice say. Jared shoves Jason aside and I can breathe again.

"I hate you," Jason tells Jared. The words are venomous and there is no doubt he means it. Jason disappears toward town.

Jared is instantly at my side. "Are you okay?" I am unable to respond as tears stream down my face. Jared pulls me close to him.

"You remembered, just now, didn't you?" Jason's voice brought me back to the moment.

"That you're a sociopath? Yeah, I remember." I glared up at him. "You said you've been searching for me."

"I have. I never got to finish what I started. You were my first taste, you know? The one that got away, you could say. I needed to find you, but *Jared* refused to tell me your name. Even when I was… ever so persuasive." His smile turned crooked. My heart ached as everything settled in. Jared had been protecting me this whole time. Tears stung my eyes. Even now, as a ghost, he tried protecting me. *He did protect me.* When I was attacked at the party, he woke me up.

"I don't understand something. If this was your plan all along, then why did you bother saving me at the party?" I knew I should be plotting my escape instead of playing twenty questions with him, but I couldn't see any way out with him right here, so my best bet to stay safe was to keep him distracted.

He let out an arrogant laugh. "Who do you think paid him to do it?"

"What? But I thought the cheerleaders…" I trailed off in befuddlement. Had I been wrong to seek revenge on the squad?

"Cindy did lace your drink with something. I just saw an opportunity I couldn't pass up."

"Opportunity for what?" My shock was obvious. He seemed pleased to have tricked me.

"To earn your trust, of course. And it worked. Well, that is, until you started poking around about my brother. Even dead, he's still ruining my plans for you." He scowled. He didn't know how true that last statement was.

"You're sick," I spat.

"Thank you." His face twisted in depraved gratification. He leaned down, quickly pressing his lips to mine. His tongue demanded access to my mouth where it forcefully explored every crevice. The metallic taste of my own blood layered my tongue. I jerked my head as far away as I could, breaking the kiss. A smile that reminded me of a picture I once saw of the Joker crept across his face. "Let's begin."

Hysteria overtook me as I threw my body wildly. His athletic build could not be outdone, though. His hands slipped around my neck, and tightened. I choked as I tried to get air into my lungs. My blocked airways were useless. Alarm filled me as black spots filled my vision. He was killing me. I was going to die because I refused to listen to Jared. My body became limp moments before I lost consciousness.

I awoke sometime after that with the same amount of confusion as the first time. But my burning throat quickly reminded me of my predicament. My eyes scanned the room. The light was on this time, but Jason was not around. I stared at the table of knives with a mix of dread and longing. I wished he had left it just a little bit closer. I was desperate for an escape plan. There was only one thing I could think of to do, but I wasn't sure I had the required core strength to pull it off.

I inhaled deeply before lifting my legs in a maneuver I could thank yoga and cheerleading for. My feet reached over my shoulders and underneath the bed frame. If I could lift it just enough, then I could slide the rope out from under the leg. I pushed with all I could muster, but the frame barely budged. Between the awkward angle and my physical state, this wasn't happening. The noises I had made must have alarmed Jason to my resurrection because I heard his footsteps. I quickly straightened myself back out before he could see what I had been doing.

"You're finally awake," he exclaimed. "You know, you take longer to come to than the others." He stepped further into the room. "The suspense is… enthralling."

He rolled the table of knives closer to me. I readied my muscles. I knew I'd only have moments to act before he'd hold down my legs again. Once he reached me, he bent down to study my wound. He never saw it coming as I lifted both legs and kicked him in the side. He flew across the room, falling into a heap near the door. I reached out with my leg and locked the table in place so it wouldn't roll away. With my other leg, I stretched as far as I could, until my foot reached the surface. I could feel the handle of a knife. My toes almost had it in their grip when Jason moved the table away. I nearly sobbed as my hope for escape wheeled away with the knives. He locked both of my ankles with just one of his hands and placed them back to the floor. I flailed violently, but it was no use. If it came down to brawn, he'd win every time. He situated himself onto my legs and leaned in close to my ear.

"Now, that's what I'm talking about." His voice dripped in sick pleasure. "That is what all the others lacked. Your fire. That's why you are perfect." He glanced down at my body. "Well, at least, you will be when I'm through with you."

I shuddered. "Why are you doing this?"

"Because I want to." His tone held an almost "duh" sentiment to it. "I've dreamed of this moment with you for so long. A desire denied to me by my own flesh and blood. The thing Jared didn't realize is that it was our destiny to be together again. He got in the way of that destiny and he lost his life for it."

Every time he mentioned Jared, I wanted to grab a knife and stab him in the heart. Who murders their own brother? It was pure evil. Especially, killing someone as caring as Jared. Fiery pits of fury flamed inside my core. I shifted my head and sank my teeth into his arm. I bit down harder than I'd ever allowed myself to bite someone in the past. He screamed out in pain before he forced my mouth off him.

There, now he was marked by his crime. When they found my body, they would match my teeth to his wound. *If they found my body,* a dark voice inside me chimed in. *They only found one body and who knew how many girls he'd actually killed?* They were merely missing. Even Jared. There were a lot of places to hide bodies in the woods.

He shoved my head to the floor. "That is *not* how this works." he scolded as he grabbed a knife. This one was short and had a bit of a curve to it. "Now, I have to punish you." My throat tightened. His warped sense of pleasure made me dread what he considered punishment. He tugged one of my legs out from under him and forced my knee to bend. He held my foot in front of his face. "Pick a toe."

"What?" Shock and alarm rattled my brain. *He can't be serious.* His expression told me he was dead serious.

"*Pick a toe,*" he commanded.

"No, please!" I wailed.

"I guess I have to pick for you." He pointed to my big toe. "Eeny." He pointed to the next one. "Meeny."

"No!" I kicked viciously, aiming for his face. He remained in complete control over my foot.

"Miny," he continued. He pointed the knife to the toe next to my pinkie. "Moe."

"Stop! I'm sorry," I begged. My heart raced inside my chest as the terror of the threat pulsed through me.

I closed my eyes as he singled out the toe. I felt the point of the knife sink into the skin on top of the toe and I let out a whimper. He circled the tip all the way around my toe until I had a ring of blood. I braced myself for the mutilation, but it never came. I peeked out from behind my eyelids. He gazed at me with a glowering expression.

"Are you going to behave?" he asked, still holding the knife to his hostage. Bleakness overcame me. I nodded. "I prefer not to cut off any body parts, but I will to make a point." His tone was dour. He moved my leg back underneath him. He shook his head as if he were shaking away the bad memory. His mood seemed to turn around just as quickly as it had when I bit him. He leered at me with a wolfish expression. The knife still lay in the palm of his hand. "Where to begin?"

He placed the blade to the side of my waist. He sliced along my ribcage only an inch or so below my bra. The cut stung, but I refused to make a sound. He seemed to get off on my reactions, so I decided I'd remain as silent as possible. His focus was solely on the mark he'd made. His tongue traced along the bloody line. He let out a heavy moan. My stomach whirled in response. I couldn't control my tears as they trickled down the sides of my face.

His eyes met mine with a yearning. He held my face with his hand as he moved his mouth near my ear. "I want to stick it in you." His voice was low and gravelly, as if he were on the verge of losing control.

"What? No! Don't!" *Was he going to rape me?* Is that what this whole thing led to? Somehow, that seemed worse than anything he'd done, thus far.

"I don't know if I can stop myself. I want it so bad." His body lowered only slightly, but I was hyper aware of it, now.

"Please, I'm a virgin. I'm begging you not to. I will do anything." The tears fell hard now. Hopelessness threatened to devour me within its deep, dark pits.

"What?" He jerked back. "No, that's not what I'm talking about." His tone almost seemed offended.

"Then, what are you talking about?" I questioned, puzzled.

"This." He lifted the knife to my line of sight.

I gulped. A strange mix of emotions flooded me. Relief that he wasn't talking about sex and terror that he wanted to stab me. I wanted to plead with him not to, but I was pretty sure that would only encourage the notion. He dragged the knife along my side, not actually pressing it into my skin. It was more of a tickle. The anticipation was almost too much to bear.

I cried out as he shoved the blade into my abdomen. Pain seared every miniscule nerve the knife grazed. Blood coated my stomach in layers of hot liquid. He removed the knife which caused another sharp pain. His fingers were a dark red as he stared down at his handiwork with great interest. I had never seen anything more disturbing. He lavished in my bleeding.

He grabbed a rag from his back pocket and wiped his hands clean. "That was…" He smirked down at me. "Satisfying. I think I need a cigarette. Or two. Lights out, Beth." His fingers laced around my neck, tightening until the world became black to me, once again.

When I regained consciousness, my stomach screamed at me in agony. I had never felt pain as intense as this before. It felt as if I'd had surgery without any medication. I glanced down to see that Jason had cleaned the wound and bandaged it.

How considerate, I thought bitterly. *Keep me alive longer so you can torture me.*

Breathing was difficult. Each breath caused a burning sensation in my throat and a searing throb to radiate from my stomach. Hopelessness settled over me. The more injured I became, the slimmer my chances of escape would be. A sob slipped through my lips before I could control it. A few seconds later, Jason entered the room.

I watched as he slid to the floor next to me. He stared at me momentarily before speaking. "I'm sorry for earlier," he said to my surprise. "I got carried away and nearly ruined everything. All this preparation and I still almost messed everything up." When I didn't respond, he continued. "To make it up to you, I'm going to give you a gift. I wasn't planning on giving you this until we were finished, but I feel like you deserve it."

He wanted to give me another gift? Now? Trepidation kept me from speaking. He lifted himself from the ground and waltzed over to the corner of the room. Tossing my dress aside, he revealed two boxes, a jewelry box and a flower box. *So, the gifts were from him.* My suspicions were correct. This meant I had worn the jewelry of his previous victims. Disgust lay heavily in the depth of my stomach and I was suddenly desperate for a shower.

"Here. I'll open it for you." He grinned. He tugged out three purple flowers. "These are statice. They mean remembrance. It seemed fitting since you finally remembered the moment we shared as children." He opened the jewelry box. I gasped at the bracelet that lay inside.

"That's Amanda's!" I yelled in outrage.

"Yes, it is." His eyes studied my face for my reaction.

"You bastard! You killed her?" Horror pierced through my words.

"I did it for you." Hurt seeped into his tone.

"What?"

"I did *all* of this for you." He gestured broadly with his hands.

"What do you mean, all of this?" My gut twisted.

"I perfected my plan on all those other girls so I'd have it right for you. I only killed Amanda to practice one last time. I've waited years to be with you again. I couldn't screw it up. Not with you," he insisted.

Darkness rushed over me as his words sank in. *This whole thing was about me?* All those girls died so he could eventually kill me. Unfounded guilt filled my chest. It wasn't my fault but somehow it was. It all boiled down to his obsession with me. My silence seemed to confuse him.

"Don't you understand? We can finally be together," he declared. He pulled out his wallet, showing me the picture that had been missing from the photo album. "It's you. It's always been you." My chest clenched as he showed me further proof that he'd been in my house.

"Be together? You're going to kill me," I asserted.

"No, I'm not! Don't you see?" His tone took on a desperation and vulnerability that left me taken aback. "I killed all those girls, so that I *wouldn't* kill you. I had to learn."

"You stabbed me!" I countered.

My brain couldn't seem to process what he was getting at. It just didn't add up. *Why are you trying to understand the ramblings of a madman?* I asked myself.

"I said I was sorry!" His voice raised in frustration.

Why are you poking the bear? I scolded myself.

"You're right. You did. I forgive you." I prayed my new approach would keep me alive. If I could appease his fantasies long enough for my aunt to notice I was missing, maybe the cops would find me in time.

His lips curled into a smile that you might see on a child. "Good. Now, let me put your gift on." He snapped the bracelet on around my forearm since the rope blocked my wrists. "Oh, and I have one more gift." He darted out of the room and returned with a dirty plastic bag. I let out a sharp gasp as I recognized it. "I dug this up for you." He tugged out the dark-haired china doll I had buried in the backyard.

"You were the one that put the doll in my bed." I spoke slowly as the realization hit me.

"You looked like you were having nightmares," he explained. I was unsure how to respond. Coming from someone else, that might have sounded like a sweet gesture. However, mixed with his hysterical behavior and his crazed eyes, it was rather disturbing. "You used to love this doll. Why did you bury it?"

I was almost embarrassed to admit my reasoning. "I thought it was haunted." My answer caused him to laugh loudly.

"I suppose it would be a tad unsettling to wake up with the doll in your bed." He sounded amused by the whole thing. I wanted to respond by telling him just how unsettling everything he'd done had been, but I thought better of it.

My panic resurfaced as Jason laid his arms across my legs. He reached for the table and grabbed what looked like a carving knife. I gulped back the vomit that threatened to make an appearance. I had considered just puking all over him, but I didn't want to risk his punishment. I closed my eyes and held my breath.

He said he wasn't going to kill me, I reminded myself. *Yeah, okay, let's trust the psychopath with a slicing fetish that just happens to be holding a knife. That sounds smart.* I quieted the battling voices in my head.

I squeezed my eyes harder when I felt the sting of the blade against my side. It carved a circular shape along my skin. The pain was too much and I couldn't concentrate enough to picture its design in my head. I became resigned to the pain which did very little to lessen it. The sickening sound of his wet tongue on my skin reached my ears long before my nerves defined the sensation. Disgust and terror paralyzed me as I lay stiffly under his touch. He was consumed with his project and paid no attention to me.

He let out a groan that signaled he was finished. When I peeked out from behind my eyelids, I caught him watching me. My muscles tensed up as he laid his head on my stomach. I was wound tight while he appeared to have never been more at ease. He placed a small kiss to my stomach and I couldn't help my instinct to suck in to avoid the contact.

His eyes met mine with a sad expression. "You'll understand when we're through. I know you will."

I couldn't stop the train of thoughts that came next. *What happens when he's done?* I couldn't pretend I wanted to be with him. I wasn't that great of an actress. Would he just kill me, then? Was it worth playing along only to be tortured and eventually killed anyway? What if the cops never found me? Would I be locked in this cabin forever? Waiting day in and day out for Jason to return and cut me some more? I couldn't even begin to fathom how he thought we were going to be together after all of this. His mind was far more diluted than I had originally thought. At least when I thought he was killing girls because he liked it, his actions were predictable. I knew that outcome. But this, I just didn't understand. Was I to be his captive for all of time? Or was he so far unhinged that he actually believed we would be some happy couple in the end?

"I'm tired," I told him in a rough voice.

"It's been a long night." He stood up. "We'll pick this up tomorrow."

I braced myself for the panic and pain that would come with being strangled. His hands slipped around my neck and my air supply was gone. My lungs demanded to be filled as my brain screamed in panic. Slowly, my vision was taken over by black spots until they converged into one big blob of darkness.

CHAPTER ELEVEN

SECRETS OF THE DEAD

"Lizzie," I heard a soft voice say. A hand brushed my face. "Lizzie, you have to get up. Jason is in the shower. This is your only chance."

My eyes flew open. Jared crouched over me with a terrified look on his face. "Jared! I'm so sorry I didn't believe you." My voice was hoarse. I briefly wondered if all the strangling was causing permanent damage.

"Later, okay? We have to get you out of here," he asserted.

I nodded. "Right. Can you hand me a knife?"

"I can't." He demonstrated this by waving his hand toward the table. It went straight through it.

"I don't understand. How can you touch *me*, then?" Disappointment siphoned at my energy. It threatened to take away my will to escape.

"I have no idea," he admitted.

"The only way I can get out is if I lift the bed with my legs, but I'm too weak." I fought off the feeling of despondence that called to me. I had to stay strong. I had to fight to survive.

"Maybe I can help," he announced.

"How?" If he couldn't touch the bed, then how could he help?

"Just place your feet under the bed frame," he ordered. I obeyed, holding in a wail as pain shot through my stomach. Once I was in position, he stood with one leg on either side of me and placed his hands on the tops of my feet. I now understood what he was doing. He couldn't touch the bed, but he could touch me. He bent his legs to brace himself. "Okay, when I say push, use every last bit of strength you have." I nodded. "Okay, go."

I strained my muscles and they scolded me in response. I felt blood seep out of my stomach wound as it throbbed from the movement. Jared joined in on my efforts, which seemed to be working. The bed frame lifted and I slid the rope out from under the bedpost. I didn't hesitate to leap to my feet. The sudden motion caused my head to spin and I became uneasy on my feet. Jared braced me until the spinning subsided. Terror that Jason would return at any moment drove me to act. I snatched a knife from the table and used it to cut through the rope that bound my hands. Once free, I used the rope to tie the knife to my outer thigh. I grabbed my dress and tugged it over my head, ignoring the sharp pain that shot through my stomach.

"How do I get out of here?" I questioned, turning to Jared.

"The bathroom is right across the hall, so you have to go out the window," Jared informed me.

Great. I scanned the room in search of my sandals. They were nowhere in sight, and I didn't have time to look harder. I crossed the room and jerked the window open. The moon was bright and cast much needed light over everything. Wow, this cabin was huge. Not only was it two stories, but the cabin itself was raised up about six feet. I was on the second floor, so there was no way I could jump without breaking my leg. I scanned the area for an alternative plan. The wall next to the window was built from brick with every other one jetting out.

"How are your wall climbing skills?" Jared asked.

"I guess we're about to find out," I muttered.

I heaved myself through the window to where I sat on the window pane. I noticed a good-sized brick sticking out near me. Ignoring the grunts of all my wounds, I twisted around and placed my foot on it. I shifted some of my weight to test its stability. It remained sturdy. I slid my arm out and grabbed hold of another brick. Carefully, I made my way down, brick by brick until both feet were safely on the ground.

"Now, run!" Jared commanded as he appeared beside me. I pushed past all my aches and pains and let adrenaline take over. I sped across the small clearing that led to the forest. I had no idea where I was going or how to get there, but I hoped I could lose Jason in the woods. I just prayed I didn't get myself completely lost in the process. "This way." Jared pointed to the left.

"Where are we going?" I questioned, not stopping to do so.

"There's a tower ranger station. It's pretty far, but it's your only hope," he told me.

Only hope. Yeah, got it. I wanted to ask how far *pretty far* was, but I knew I wouldn't like the answer, so I kept my mouth shut.

I was probably half a mile from the cabin when I heard a loud roar. *Jason knows I'm gone.* Jared gave me a worried look, and I picked up my pace. I had some distance on Jason, but he had no injuries to contend with. After another half hour, exhaustion was wearing me thin. It was late and pain was reacquainting itself with me. I glanced down to my midsection and noticed blood had soaked through my bandage and seeped through my dress.

"I need to stop." My voice was breathless as I doubled over in pain.

"You can't." Jared laid his hand on my shoulder. "He's looking for you."

"The pain is too much. I need a break," I pled.

His eyes moved to my bleeding torso before he nodded. "I know a place you can hide out for a bit."

I sighed in relief. I followed behind Jared but made it only a few more steps before falling to my knees. I suppressed a groan, but it still bubbled up around the constriction of my throat.

"I'm going to try to carry you." Jared placed one of my arms around his neck as he lifted me against his chest. I clutched his shirt as another sharp pain shot through me. He carried me for about five minutes before my body suddenly fell through his arms.

"What happened?" I asked, lifting myself

from the ground.

"I guess I can only hold you for short periods of time." Jared reached around my waist to help me up. "We're almost there."

I wobbled along, leaning my body weight into Jared as we made our way to a dense set of trees.

"This is it," Jared said.

"What?" I glanced around, unsure of what I was supposed to be seeing. He pointed up. My eyes followed the trees until I noticed a small, wooden hideout. "How'd you know that was there?"

"My dad used to take me hunting in these woods. That's his," Jared explained.

"If it's your dad's, then Jason knows about it," I pointed out.

"No, Jason never went hunting with us. Hunting wasn't his thing," he said.

"Seriously?" I scoffed. "Hunting animals, maybe."

He shrugged. "You'll have to grab that rope to pull down the ladder."

"I'm not sure I can climb that high," I said warily.

"It's the safest place for you to rest," Jared asserted.

I nodded and tugged on the rope. Just as Jared said, the rope ladder tumbled down. I climbed the ladder, pushing through the searing pain. Jared was already in the little makeshift tree house and helped lift me into it. I pulled the ladder in after me.

I collapsed against Jared. I was too tired to move, so I merely shifted to the side of him. The little shack was not meant for a person to lie in, so space was limited. I curled up to Jared's side but glanced up at him to make sure it was all right. He slipped his arm around my hips careful not to touch my wound and tugged me closer. Relief poured through me for various reasons. I was glad to be out of that cabin. I was thrilled that Jared wasn't mad at me for doubting him. Unfortunately, all my relief was laced with the terror that Jason would catch me. I shuddered.

"Thanks for coming for me," I whispered into his chest. "I know I didn't deserve it after leaving you the way I did."

"I can't blame you for the way you reacted. I wouldn't have believed me, either," he admitted.

"So, you really are..." I couldn't even finish the sentence. My throat tightened as tears threatened to spill over.

"Dead? Yes," he said sadly. His confirmation was too much. I let out a sob as the tears streamed down my face. He pulled me tighter against him.

"It doesn't even matter. Soon, I'll be joining you in the afterlife." I choked on a humorless laugh.

He lifted my chin so I was looking at him. "Not if I can help it, you're not," he asserted.

"What can you possibly do?"

"I know these woods better than anyone. Even Jason. I can guide you to safety." His tone sounded determined.

"If I don't bleed out first." My heart rate sped up at the sight of so much blood. Worry etched itself on Jared's face. We were silent for a moment as our individual thoughts held us hostage.

"Why didn't you tell me the truth sooner?" I asked him.

Shame covered his handsome face. "I thought if I could keep you away from Jason, then you'd be safe." He paused, glancing away. "I should have told you to leave, but I was being selfish. I wanted to be near you."

"I wouldn't have believed you, then, either," I admitted.

"I still should have tried." He seemed to

scold himself before falling silent. After a moment, he whispered, "Get some sleep. I'll wake you when it's time to go."

I folded my arms underneath my head. Despite the pain, it didn't take long for sleep to claim me. My fatigue could no longer be ignored.

The creek is back, as well as the tree. Jared leans against the tree with an unsure expression.

"Is it alright that I'm here?" he asks me. I understand his trepidation. During my last dream, I sent him away.

"I'm glad you're here," I tell him. I lie under the shade of the tree and, a moment later, Jared joins me. "So, it's always been you? In my dreams?" I ask, needing to hear him confirm it one last time.

"Yes." He slides his hand into mine, interlocking our fingers. "Does that make you uncomfortable? My being in your dreams?"

"No. You would have been in them anyway," I admit with a smile. My answer seems to lighten his mind. He wraps me in his arms as he places a small kiss on my forehead. Any pain I might have been expecting never came. I realize I am not hurting in my dream.

Boldness seeps into me. I might be dying out there in the woods. I'm not about to play it safe. I draw his mouth to mine. My lips are fervent as they move with his. Need and passion consumes us as we press into each other. He sighs against my mouth in either contentment or longing. Perhaps, both.

"If I die, then we can be together," I remark.

His face falls instantly.

"That's not what I want." He frowns down at me.

Hurt tears at my heart.

"You don't want to be with me?" I ask.

"Not at the cost of your life. I am doing everything I can to keep you alive. Please, don't give up on me now." His blue eyes plead with me to see reason.

"You're right." I shake my head. "That was stupid. I don't want to die."

"I know." He brushes hair from my eyes as he stares down at me. More pain than I could ever understand lingers within his gaze.

"Jason said you wouldn't tell him who I was," I prompted.

"I would never do that to you." Jared traces a finger along my jawline. "He was obsessed, is still obsessed with you. I know Jason better than anyone else, even our parents. I'm the only one who's seen the monster that lives inside him."

"What did he do to you? When you wouldn't tell him?" I ask.

His eyes glance away from mine. "It doesn't matter. He never got what he wanted out of me." He sighs before moving his eyes back to mine. "I wanted to reach out to you so many times over the years, but I was afraid he'd find you. I was going to wait until I left for college, but..." He doesn't finish the thought. We both know what comes after that but. He died. My chest feels constricted again. Breathing takes deep concentration as I feel a panic attack seeking to take hold. My future is unknown. I may or may not survive this, but at least I have a chance. Jared doesn't. He is already dead. It isn't fair.

"I'm sorry," I whimper softly.

"None of this is your fault," he assures as he caresses my cheek.

"Where did he leave your body? I'll make sure your parents find it," I say adamantly.

"I'm not worried about that right now." His smile is sad.

"What do you think it means that you can touch me and no one else?" My change in subject seems to throw him off guard for a moment.

"I think maybe our souls are connected, somehow," he speculates.

"Like soulmates?" I conclude from his statement. His expression tells me that's exactly what he means but is too unsure of my reaction to say it. Vulnerability is clear in his blue eyes. I reach up and brush back his single curl that has fallen into his face. "That makes sense."

"I wish everything could be different." He bites his lip as his eyes soak me in. "I wish we could have been

together. Even if it had only been a short time."

"Maybe…" I trail off. I cannot bring myself to say what I'm thinking.

"What?" he encourages.

"If I survive, or maybe even if I don't, but after this, maybe we can be together." I hold my breath for his reaction. His eyes tell me this is not a new thought for him.

"We can't. If you survive this, the last thing you should do is hold onto a ghost," he asserts. "You have to live your life. Otherwise, this will all be for naught."

I throw my arms around him. "We can make it work. I don't want a life without you in it. Please." The last word is more of a sob.

"And what kind of life would that be? Living in dreams? That's not what you truly want. You deserve so much more than that," he coaxes.

"It's not fair. We didn't even get a chance." My voice sounds petulant, but I do not care.

"I know." His voice is solemn, as if this is something he has thought about often.

We lie wrapped in each other, soaking in the essence of one another for a long while. Neither of us seem to want to let the moment go. More questions linger in my mind and I soon cannot contain it another second.

"Why didn't I tell anyone about what Jason did?" I ask him.

"I don't know. The next day, you were bandaged up

and you acted like you couldn't even remember what had happened," he tells me.

"Why didn't you say anything to me?" I'm not angry but simply curious.

"I thought it was better that you didn't remember. I know if something like that had happened to me, I would much rather not remember," he explains. I nod at his reasoning.

"So, I've heard a lot of rumors about you... and Vegas?" I say.

"Yeah..." he says sheepishly. "It's probably all true, minus the running away part."

"So, you're a math genius that can count cards?" I smile as his face turns slightly red.

"It got me into a lot of trouble, but I stopped with all of that," he replies.

We're quiet for a small stretch of time. I build up the courage to ask what I have been wanting to all night.

"Will you tell me about the night you died? If you feel comfortable with it, that is." I watch his face for hints of unease. They are there, but are soon replaced with sadness. I almost take it back, but then he answers.

"I always knew my brother had an evil side. He'd never bothered hiding that part of himself from me. He'd broken many of my bones as children, telling our parents it was an accident," he begins. Guilt flushes my system. That must have been Jason's form of persuasion to get my name.

Jared continues, "I never thought that he could actually kill someone, though. It was last summer. I came to the cabin for some alone time to clear my head. I was surprised to see that Jason was there. I thought he might've had the same idea. It was late, so I went straight for my bedroom to crash. That's when I found her. She looked a lot like you, only a little different. He had her tied up. Her entire body was covered in cuts. She'd been stabbed multiple times. She asked me to help her. So, I did. We ran from Jason in the forest. He chased us down with a crossbow. He aimed it at her, so I stepped in the way. He shot me in the chest. I lived only long enough to see her shot down, as well." His voice is tight as he recounts the story. "I couldn't save her."

"But you tried," I console.

"It doesn't matter. I couldn't save her and I can't save you." His words are sharp as if he wishes to slice his own mouth on them.

"It does matter," I declare. "You were willing to give your life for a complete stranger. Your brother's soul is dark and twisted, but your soul is beautiful and perfect. If I can survive this, I hope that gives you the peace you've so long deserved." I place my hand on his cheek.

"If you survive, my death will be worth it."

CHAPTER TWELVE

SECRETS NEVER STAY BURIED

"Lizzie, it's time to wake up. We have to get moving." Jared's voice drew me back to the living. My body felt ten times worse now than it did before I slept. My stomach wound felt raw while the rest of my body simply ached. I glanced out of the shack and saw the sun peeking just barely above the horizon.

"Is he still out there?" I hoped that Jason had given up and left. I knew this was the least likely thing he could do, short of growing a tail and changing his name to *Cyan Pepper*.

"Yes, but he's headed in a different direction. That's why we should leave now." Jared tugged at my arm. After the painful descent from the hideout, I stumbled after Jared. My mind didn't feel as groggy, but my body seemed to hate me. My throat was sore, my cuts burned with possible infections, and my stomach began bleeding, once more. I could tell Jared was concerned over my blood loss by the anxious glances he was shooting at my stomach.

The pain slowly turned into numbness. This caused me more panic than the worst of the pain ever did. My body was shutting down. My alarm caused my footing to falter and I stumbled forward. I grabbed the closest thing within arm's reach which happened to be a low hanging branch. Unfortunately, it was not a sturdy one and broke off. My body tumbled to the ground along with the rather large branch. An ear-splitting thump reverberated throughout the forest. Jared froze staring down at me with wide eyes.

"Do you think he heard that?" My heart pounded anxiously in my chest.

"Let me check." Jared disappeared for a moment before reappearing. "Yes, he did."

Jared tugged me to my feet with an urgency that was stemmed by fear. Pain shot through my ankle. I must have twisted it when I fell. In the fastest speed we could manage with me leaning on Jared, we raced to our destination.

"Beth!" I heard Jason's voice boom across the forest. My fear tripled at the realization that he was within earshot. I wasn't going to make it.

"Ignore him and just keep going," Jared

coaxed.

"Come back now and I won't punish you!" Jason screamed out.

My throat constricted at the thought of losing a toe. If that was even where he'd stop. He had wanted to remove a toe when I bit him. What would he do for this? I shook off my panic and focused on increasing my speed.

"How much further?" I whispered to Jared.

"It's just right up here," he said to my relief.

We stepped into a clearing that held a large tower right smack in the middle. I gulped as I realized how far I'd have to climb to reach the top. With no time to lose, I hurried to the ladder and began my ascent. What might have taken five minutes, took me at least ten with all my injuries. Once I finally reached the top, I dashed to the radio. Jared watched as I fumbled with the buttons.

"This one." He pointed out the correct knob.

"Hello? Is anyone there?" I screeched into the radio.

"This is central station. Who am I speaking with?" A voice crackled over the radio. I could have cried with relief.

"My name is Elizabeth Michaels. I was kidnapped by a boy named Jason…" I glanced to Jared for the missing information.

"Knight," he answered.

"Jason Knight. He is trying to kill me. I need help." I spoke quickly.

"Beth!" Jason's voice caused my heart to cease its beating as I became paralyzed with fear.

"Elizabeth. We are sending help now. We need you to stay there," the voice informed me, placing me back in control of my body.

"I can't. He's coming." My voice shook in terror.

I rushed out on the balcony of the tower to see how far Jason was.

"I'm going to run for it," I told Jared.

"He's too close. You need to hide. Then, attack with that knife you brought," Jared ordered.

I nodded, knowing his plan was the best bet. I glanced down to see Jason had begun climbing the ladder. I met Jared's eyes and unspoken words seemed to pass between us. This could be my last moments alive. Without any hesitation, Jared drew my mouth to his in a deep kiss that made me forget all the horror that was happening. I wanted to soak up every ounce of him, but Jason would be to the top soon.

I ducked down near the door to the station tower, knife in hand. I would only get one shot and I knew I had to be merciless. I heard his feet hit the balcony outside. His footsteps crept closer to the door. I was ready. The moment he stepped past the threshold, I lunged at him. He seemed shocked but quickly grabbed my wrist. He jerked my arm, forcing me to fling the knife off the tower.

"Nice try." Jason smirked. I cried out as I became despondent. "Come on. We're going home," he ordered. I knew he didn't mean to take me to my home. He meant the cabin. Jared attempted to punch Jason, but his fist went right through him. Fury washed over Jared's face in his helplessness.

"Elizabeth? Are you still there?" said the voice over the speaker.

Jason's eyes narrowed. "What have you done?" His voice was low and cold. I felt an icy shiver run up my spine. "Now, we have to die."

"What?" I squeaked.

"Why did you have to do that?" His eyes were filled with sorrow as he laced his hands around my neck. His expression told me I would not be waking up this time. I punched and kicked, but he managed to get me on my back. My head became dizzy. "This is the only way we can be together now." Jason's words wrapped themselves around my brain and replayed over and over again.

"Stop!" I heard Jared scream. I was grateful for his efforts, but there was nothing he could do. Except, I wasn't the only one who heard Jared. Jason's head shot up as his face drained of color.

"I killed you," Jason asserted. "How is this possible?"

"Get away from her!" Jared demanded.

"You will *not* ruin this moment for me!" Jason barked.

He released his hold on my neck and I gasped for air instantly. He surged after Jared, who stood near the edge. Jason's arms were extended as if to grab Jared. Only, Jared could not be grabbed. Jason ran right through Jared and tumbled over the edge.

I screamed in horror as Jared rushed over to me. I couldn't bring myself to verify that Jason was dead with a glance over the edge. Jared checked for me and nodded solemnly. I sobbed in relief.

"Lizzie, your stomach." Jared's face turned ashen as he stared down. I glanced at my now red dress. The wound had opened back up and was bleeding profusely. That was when I realized my dizziness never ceased. I was losing too much blood. Numbness made its way through my body. The booming sound of a chopper filled the air. "You just have to hold on a little bit longer, okay?"

I nodded. Jared grasped my hand as he stared into my eyes. I inhaled sharply as his face began to fade in and out.

"Jared, what's happening?"

"I don't know. I'm being pulled some-where." His eyes were wide. Tears filled mine at the thought of him leaving. "I think I'm moving on."

"Please, don't go!" I yelled selfishly. "Stay."

"I wish I knew how." He shook his head. "Lizzie, I love you."

"I love you, too." No sooner were the words out of my mouth than his entire form vanished altogether. My tears were now falling with a force I could not control. My numbness did not extend to my emotions. Although, I desperately wished it did. A void, so desolate and so empty, I cannot imagine anything alive capable of surviving its depths, called to me like a siren. The need to fall into its nothingness was overpowering and I let myself go. Emptiness washed over me with all of its glorious nothing-ness. Everything ceased to exist. *I* ceased to exist.

I awoke to bright lights that burned my eyes. A familiar face filled my view as a worried expression covered every inch of it. My mother's mouth moved, but my mind couldn't follow her words. My brain raced to put together the events that led me to this moment. Suddenly, one face was brought to the forefront of my mind and I wanted nothing more than to see it one last time. *Jared was gone.* Something hollow ebbed at me from the inside.

I turned over on my side and ignored what-ever it was my mother said. I closed my eyes, praying Jared would be there. *Nothing.* My face became damp with new tears. If I couldn't have Jared, then I didn't want to be here. I gave into the tugging that had been relentless since I became conscious. I desired the void and everything it had to offer. I drifted back into the pits of nothingness.

This was my new home now.

I had no sense of time as my eyelids opened, once again. Despair hit me almost instantly and I reached for that void to save me. A voice rang through my mind before I could reach my saving grace. *You have to live your life. Otherwise, this will all be for naught.* Jared had said that to me. Was I spitting on his sacrifices by choosing to live in my safe haven? I knew the answer to that. He never wanted that for me. I was being selfish. *I'm alive and he's dead.* I needed to be more appreciative. But how could I move on?

Maybe, I didn't need to move on. I just needed to wake up.

This time when I opened my eyes, they remained open. I scanned the empty hospital room. A quick glance at the clock on the wall and the dark window told me it was in the middle of the night, but I had no way to tell how many days I'd been here. I wondered where my mother had gone but found I wasn't too concerned. My room door was open, but the hallways were nearly silent, save for a few shuffling sounds made by the nurses on duty.

I listened intently to see if I could hear my mother's voice. I only heard whispered conversations held by the nurses. I had given up listening in when a couple of nurses began speaking near my door.

"It's remarkable is what it is," one nurse commented.

"Can you imagine? Waking up from a coma after so long? Barely even remembering your own name? Poor thing," the second nurse said.

Something about their conversation struck a chord in me. I felt compelled to leave my hospital room in search of… well, I wasn't quite sure what I was in search of, but I knew it was important.

I waited for the nurses to move along before tip-toeing out into the hall. I'd never been to this hospital before in my life, yet something was telling me I needed to go right. As if I were being guided by my spirit alone, I found myself in front of another hospital room door.

"Will he ever recover his memories?" I heard a weeping woman ask from around the corner.

"There's just no way to know. They might come back tomorrow or they may never come back," an official sounding voice replied.

I ignored their conversation and slipped into the room. A curtain blocked my view of the hospital bed. I knew this was incredibly inappropriate, but I just could not stop myself. I tugged the curtain aside and nearly fell to my knees at the sight.

Jared lay in the bed. Alive and breathing. My hands shook as my brain raced. *This can't be real. Jared is dead. He told me so.* Yet, here he was. I felt myself being dragged closer to him as if we were magnets. I needed to touch him. I needed to feel that this was real.

I reached my hand out and traced a finger along his jaw. I ran it under his nose to feel his warm breath against my skin. I was so terrified to allow hope, but nothing about this seemed to be anything other than legit. Jared was alive. I pressed my palm to his cheek which seemed to stir him. His eyelids fluttered open. His bright blue eyes met mine. I let my hand fall to my side as I felt unsure of what to do.

"Hi." His voice was raspy as if he were speaking through a dry throat.

"Hi." It was all I could seem to muster.

"Do I know you?" He cocked his head to the side as if in deep thought.

My heart dropped. *He doesn't remember.* My mind replayed the conversation I overheard in the hallway. *He may never get back his memories.* My mind raced with what to say. Do I tell him what happened? Would he think I was crazy?

"Elizabeth, right?" His words settled inside me.

"Yeah," I answered. I was about to tell him when something else he had told me whispered through my mind. *I know if something like that had happened to me, I would much rather not remember.* How could I tell him when I knew for a fact he wouldn't want to be reminded? His brother tried to murder him. That shouldn't be something he had to remember.

"You have to stay away from Jason. He's obsessed with you." His eyes were filled with alarm.

"I will. I promise." I couldn't keep the sadness from my voice. I felt as if Jared were being ripped away from me all over again.

"Are you okay?" Concern etched his perfect features and I felt my heart break into two.

"Yeah, I better get back to my room, though. Get better." I turned to leave.

"Wait, what happened to you?" He gestured toward my bandages. His question left me without an answer. How could I explain what happened to me without bringing up Jason?

"Animal attack," I told him.

"Why were you all the way out here?" He frowned. This hospital was small and its location meant it nearly completely catered to the forest occupants.

"Camping." I smiled. I think he was trying to say something else, but I waved goodbye and left before he could. As I exited the room, my heart clenched so tight, I thought I might double over. I took a few deep breaths before returning to my room. Inside, my mother was speaking harshly to one of the nurses, presumably for losing me.

"There you are! Where did you go, young lady?" My mom's voice was hard but had the edgings of worry. The nurse took the opportunity to jet out of the room. I couldn't blame him.

"I'm sorry. I was looking for you," I lied.

"Oh, baby. I'm so sorry I wasn't here when you woke up. I just needed to stretch my legs a little. Come, lay down." She maneuvered me back to bed. "How are you feeling? Do you need more pain medicine?"

"No, I'm fine." I waved off her fretting.

"Well, I need to tell you that when we leave the hospital, you're moving back home," she informed me.

"*Mom*," I argued.

"Before you say anything, you agreed that one more mishap and you would move back. Even aside from that, you were *kidnapped* and nearly *killed*. There is no way I am leaving you in Middleton," she asserted.

I took a calming breath before speaking. "I understand your fears, but Jason is dead. He can't hurt me or anyone else. I am nearly an adult.

Please, let me make this decision."

"Beth…"

"Mom, please," I begged.

"You almost died." Her eyes were full of tears now. "Even after they brought you here, they were saying you had lost too much blood. I thought I was going to lose you and I was stuck in a car driving for nine hours."

"I know, Mom. I'm *really* sorry, but I don't want to leave Middleton," I asserted. "I'll be eighteen in a month. This should be my decision."

My mom's cheeks were wet with tears. I hadn't seen her cry in years. Then, she did something even more astonishing. Something I had never seen her do. She caved without a fight. She nodded her head in resignation.

CHAPTER THIRTEEN

ONE LAST SECRET

I stood at the edge of the creek watching the water sparkle in the evening sun. A chilly November breeze caressed my face causing a slight shiver of my muscles. Two months had passed since Jason's death. My decision to remain in Middleton had not been easy to follow through on. The aftermath of everything was a bit overwhelming. Questions were thrown at me from every direction. Everyone treated me with kid gloves. Only in the last week have things seemed to finally be blowing over. I couldn't wait to become invisible, once again.

I released a sigh of pent up anxiety. Jared was apparently recovering in some clinic a couple hundred miles away. I only knew this from the rumors around school. I hadn't actually heard a peep from him since I left him in that hospital room. The memory twisted in my gut until it turned into one massive knot.

It was the right thing to do, I reminded myself. He sacrificed his happiness time and again for me. I could do it for him. It was a hard truth to swallow, though. While I was elated he was alive, it ripped me apart not to be with him. It was as if my soul was missing a chunk out of it.

I glanced down at the newest portion of my tattoo. It was the final piece, actually. I spent the month before my eighteenth birthday deciding exactly what I wanted to do about my scars. Everyone told me I should get plastic surgery to remove them, but that didn't feel like the right decision. I didn't want to just pretend like nothing ever even happened.

It did happen.

So, I decided to transform the ugly memory into something beautiful. The pink scars were now green vines that wrapped around my side and swooped into a blooming flower right over the largest one on my stomach. Somehow, the tattoo gave me more closure than the month of therapy had.

My mind wandered back to the letter I had received in the mail today. I was accepted to the University of Florida. It was great news. Really, it was. Yet, the thought of moving so far from Jared gave me sharp pains deep in my chest. It seemed that step would force me to squash any hope that remained. *If there was any hope left by that point.* If Jared didn't have his memories back by now, it seemed unlikely that they would ever return. I knew that was the best thing for him. To remain blissfully unaware of the horrors he'd faced over the last year.

I stepped forward and, slipping my sandals off, grazed the surface of the creek with my toes. The water felt icy and the sensation caused my skin to prickle with goosebumps.

"You're not going to jump in, are you?" I heard a familiar voice say from behind me.

I twisted around to see Jared. My heart leapt in my chest but sank as I remembered I had to feign ignorance.

"No, it's freezing," I answered.

"I didn't think the cold bothered water sprites," he replied.

"You always used to call me that when we were children," I commented, returning my eyes to the creek. It hurt too much to look at him and not be able to wrap him in my arms. "I thought you were at some clinic."

"They finally let me out." He paused. "So, did you change your mind?"

"About what?" I stared down at my feet as

the cold grass laced itself between my toes.

"Us." His voice held a thinly veiled vulnerability.

My heart skipped a beat as a tiny glimmer of hope peeked its head out of hiding. "What do you mean?"

"You left. At the hospital. You never came back." Hurt shimmered in his blue eyes.

I still wasn't sure what he was saying. Did he remember? I didn't know how to be subtle, so I went with blunt. "Did you get your memories back?"

"I remember everything. It all came back to me later that day, but you had left. No one would let me make phone calls. I hoped you'd visit me, but you never came." He glanced away, letting a moment of silence fall over us. "It's okay if you changed your mind. I get it."

My mind stuttered. It couldn't process what he was telling me. He seemed to take my silence as an answer to a question my brain hadn't even registered yet. He nodded slowly and turned to leave. Finally, my brain began functioning at normal speeds. *He remembered.* And he was leaving. He thought I didn't want to be with him. My legs sprang to life as I let go of any suppression I had placed on my urge to run into his arms.

Erica Lee Cooke

I darted in front of him. I gazed up to meet a questioning gleam in his eyes. I grabbed the collar of his shirt and tugged him down into a kiss. Our mouths moved fervently against each other as the kiss increased in intensity. One of Jared's hands wrapped itself in my hair as the other settled against my lower back, pressing me closer. Two months' worth of yearning devoured any sense of self-control. Pure elation shot through every nerve in my body. Our breaths were heavy when we finally pulled apart.

"I didn't change my mind," I muttered.

"Why did you leave?" he whispered.

"You didn't remember any of it. It would have been selfish to remind you of all that hurt," I explained.

"If I had to remember a thousand moments of pain to hold onto *one* moment with you, I'd take that deal any day." His eyes held mine hostage and I knew he meant every word. My eyes watered with relief. I threw my arms around him, tugging him into a tight hug.

"I thought I'd lost you forever," I mumbled into his chest. "I'm sorry I didn't come visit you in the hospital. I honestly thought that's what you would've wanted."

"It's okay," he soothed.

I shifted back to see his face. His smile was so genuine and pure, it caused a thought to form in my mind. Jason and Jared really were like night and day. The Knight brothers: one dark and one light.

"Guess what?" Jared traced a finger along my jaw.

"What?"

"We're both alive." He grinned down at me.

"I know. What are the odds of that?" I ran my hands up his arms to lace around his neck.

"Well, you're the mathlete here," he teased.

"Only until you come back, Mr. Team Captain," I reminded.

He shook his head. "No, I think I need to keep a little distance between math and myself for a while."

"Well, the team will be disappointed to hear that," I commented. "So, how are you going to explain knowing so much about what's been happening with everyone this last year?"

"I've been thinking about that, and I've come up with the perfect explanation." He leaned in. "I'll tell everyone I developed psychic abilities while in my coma. You know, like from *The Dead Zone*."

I rolled my eyes and let out a laugh. "You

know, I don't think I realized your level of nerd when I kissed you. I'm not sure I can actually be seen with you at school," I teased.

"Well, that's too bad, considering we'll be in school together for another four years." His eyes seemed to glow with excitement.

"What are you talking about?" I lifted a brow.

"While I've been trying to kick my stalking habits, this seemed like a slight relapse was needed." He grinned. I gave him a look of impatience which caused him to chuckle. "I got into the University of Florida."

"Seriously?" I squealed. "So, we're going to college together?"

"I mean, if that's alright with you." He studied my face for my reaction. Instead of answering him verbally, I tugged him into another kiss. "I'll take that as a yes." He laughed.

"That's a yes." I grinned. "I'm not sure how I'm going to explain to my mom that I'm moving away with the brother of the guy who tried to kill me, but I guess we'll cross that bridge when we come to it."

"Well, I'm not my brother," he affirmed.

I glanced up and was startled to see his eyes turn to a smoky blue. I was taken aback by their resemblance to Jason's eyes. *They were brothers, after all,* I reminded myself. He seemed to notice my reaction.

"What's wrong?" he asked.

"Nothing."

Erica Lee Cooke

ABOUT THE AUTHOR

Erica Lee Cooke grew up in the small town of Bridgeport, TX. As the oldest sibling of six, she became a great storyteller, and as her imagination grew, she began to put on plays with her brothers, sisters, and various cousins as cast members. With few quiet moments at home, she did not truly begin to discover her love of reading until school, but once she did, there was no stopping her. Soon, reading stories was not enough, so she started putting pen to paper and wrote her very first book at the age of nine. Although it was never published, she proudly paraded it for all her family and friends to read. She attributes her story ideas to her extremely vivid dreams. She is currently working on the second book to *The Eyes of a Phantom Trilogy* while concurrently working on her series *Supernaturally Bound*.

For more information about Erica's books, visit
www.EricaLeeCooke.com
&
Follow Erica on Twitter @ericaleecooke
Follow Erica on Instagram @ericaleecooke
Happy reading ☺

The Eyes of a Phantom Book Two:

The Eyes to the Soul

Elizabeth Michaels is finally graduating high school, an accomplishment after the year she's had. It's only been four months since her boyfriend, Jared, moved to Florida to attend University, but it feels like an eternity. Of course, that's all about to be in the past. They have the entire summer to spend together.

Well, that was the plan, at least. Jared is offered a summer internship in Florida. The disappointing news turns into an opportunity when Jared suggests she spend the summer with him in his new company apartment.

Beth is excited about the fresh start this will bring. Especially since her overbearing mother disapproves of her relationship with Jared, considering who his brother was. What her mother doesn't understand is that Jared is nothing like his brother.

However, Beth's faith in him is tested when his behavior turns odd and erratic. Her mother's continued insistence that he shares Jason's evil nature only adds fuel to her suspicions. As much as she tries to deny it, Jared is changing. Beth is determined to hold onto the Jared that saved her life, but how long can she grasp at old memories before the present sends her a reality check?

Erica Lee Cooke